THE OTHER SIDE

THE OTHER SIDE

SERIES OF SHORT STORIES

Eileen Mcneal

ARPress
45 Dan Road Suite 5
Canton MA 02021

Hotline: 1(888) 821-0229
Fax: 1(508) 545-7580

Ordering Information:

Quantity sales. Special discounts are available on quantity purchases by corporations, associations, and others. For details, contact the publisher at the address above.

Printed in the United States of America.

ISBN-13:   Paperback   978-8-89676-222-5
                eBook   979-8-89676-223-2

Library of Congress Control Number: 2024925151

Contents

ACKNOWLEDGEMENTS

THANKS TO MY brother Wesley Cherry, Uncle Dick and Aunt Rebecca Calloway. I also thank my dear sister Marjorie Reed and loving brother Charles (Skeeter) Cherry who have gone on to heaven. Each story in the book pertains to some person or event from real life. Thanks to my daughter Valerie Martinenko, sons Mark McNeal and Michael McNeal for inspiring some of the stories and for cheering me on whenever I got discouraged.

I'm dedicating this book to my mother, Bertella Cherry, whose integrity passed on to me gave me the talent to write this book.

A FORTUNE COOKIE

JACKIE PEERED VAINLY through the windshield, struggling to see around the sheets of rain battering her car. Yes, that light blinking, was definitely a restaurant. She swerved suddenly, turning into the parking lot. The white Toyota behind her bleated an angry warning, as he swept by barely missing her tail lights. Jackie sighed. A dull ache began at the back of her neck and slowly worked its way up to her forehead. Above her head the sign flickered on and off advertising the Chang Hi Restaurant. Her stomach gave a plaintive rumble, reminding Jackie that she hadn't eaten all day. Wearily she grabbed her purse and stepped out into the blinding rain.

Globs of mud spattered her nylons as she hurried through the flooded parking lot. A potent smell of incense assaulted her nose as she spotted a booth and sank tiredly into a seat. All the tables had immaculate white tablecloths, and were neatly set with a crisp napkin and a cup and saucer. Immediately a waitress approached carrying a menu and a pot of tea.

"You have some tea and I be back to take your order," she said and then tottered away on tiny, bound feet. Only then did Jackie look around. The restaurant was practically empty. She spotted only four other people, and they looked as despondent as her.

In the corner sat a dark-skinned man in a wrinkled old raincoat. In his hand he clutched a worn five-dollar bill. The same five-dollar bill she'd dropped in his hat yesterday. No wonder he looked familiar. He was the homeless guy she passed on Fifth and Main every day at lunch time. Peculiar, that he'd picked this particular restaurant to eat in and on Christmas Eve. Unless it was providence showing her future. Yesterday she'd had one, but as of nine o' clock this morning, she'd been down sized. In a couple of weeks thought Jackie I might be as homeless as he.

Directly across from Jackie sat a tall statuesque woman. Her head was bent low, and she seemed to be crying. Her long red hair dripped rainwater on the spotless white tablecloth as she used the table napkins to wipe her eyes and catch the worse of the droplets. She wore only a red vinyl jacket and a short red skirt which barely covered her thighs. On her naked legs perched a pair of three-inch heels. Suddenly she shivered and vainly tried to warm her hands on the teapot. When she caught Jackie looking at her, she defiantly smoothed back her frazzled hair and crossed her legs. She stared back at Jackie angrily unaware tears were still clinging to her lashes.

Directly behind the redhead sat a tall executive type tapping his cup impatiently. When the waitress approached he called angrily, What have you got to drink?"

"We have coffee and best mint tea anywhere," she answered.

"No, no", he blustered. "I mean a real drink. You know, whiskey." "Oh no, no whiskey here. You have a pot of tea. I be right back, and she scurried away.

Bill rubbed his head wearily. What a day. Three months he'd gone without a drink but today had been just too much. His ex-wife had remarried today. He could understand her wanting to start a new life. Somehow though he'd always thought she still be waiting when he recovered. Now all he wanted was a drink, and he stopped at the only restaurant in town that didn't serve liquor. Impatiently he looked out the window. Thunder rumbled threateningly and lightening flashed, lighting the entire restaurant. Bill flinched back in his chair. He hated storms. Better to stay here and wait this one out.

Along the wall of the restaurant were several booths. From where Jackie sat, she was able to view one other person in the restaurant. A tall, skinny, young man sat clothed in a Santa Claus suit. He had removed his hat and beard and was staring morosely at the saltshaker in front of him.

Mark sipped his won ton soup and looked around. He'd been in this town three months searching for his sister. Since Thanksgiving he'd been playing Santa Claus to replenish his depleted resources. Two long years, he trekked from town to town tracking his sister since she ran away from home. As children, they had both been abused and mistreated by their parents, but he had escaped and eventually secured a job and finally a decent place or them both to live. When he'd returned home to rescue his sister, she'd already given up and ran away. Now he was forced to desert her again, as he could no longer afford to search for her. Mark took a sip of soup and choked as he caught a glimpse of the tall red head on the other side. From this angle she strongly favored her sister. Of course, his sister wouldn't be caught dead in an outfit like that, and he could barely discern the face under all those layers of makeup, and that ghastly colored hair. No, that poor creature was definitely not his sister.

In the silent restaurant the thunder rumbled louder and louder increasing in intensity until suddenly a sizzling streak of light erupted through the windows, and complete and total darkness fell. In the quiet blackness no one moved. Then from the entrance doors, two flickering lights appeared and then two more. They glided along to the huge table placed in the center and stopped. It was the waitresses' holding candles. When all the candles were in place, the tiny waitress turned to the diners and said, "We not going to close but if everyone sit at this table, we can serve much easier. Electric off, but most food already prepared. We see that you have good dinner. Maybe not what you order, but very good. Now everyone sits here and I be back with food."

One by one they filed to the table. Five lost souls on Christmas Eve. The tall red head called Angie reached the table first. Self-consciously she tugged at her skirt, twisted her damp hair into a bun, then sat rigidly in place. Next came homeless Harry. He sat next to Angie, unaware of the smoldering look she cast his way. She took a small vial of perfume from the satchel she carried and deliberately sprayed it in Harry's direction. Harry, however, was staring at Jackie who had just sat down opposite him. Next to Jackie sat Bill who was still griping about a drink. At the end of the table sat Mark doing his turtle imitation. He had replaced the Santa hat and scrunched way down in his seat.

Harry raised one ragged sleeve and gestured at Jackie, "What are you doing here on Christmas Eve?" he asked. "You're way too classy for this joint." Jackie flushed, "I just stopped in to have dinner. It seemed like a nice place." "Sure it is," Harry retorted. "But why aren't you home with your family?"

Jackie tugged nervously at her earring. "I—I don't have a family," she stuttered.

Bill stopped muttering to himself and focused on Harry.

"Hey, old man, leave the lady alone. We're all just here to eat. How do you know this lady, anyhow?"

Harry straightened his shoulders and faced Bill. He was aware that his pants smelled of dog urine and his shirt reeked of stale wine. The five dollars he clutched in his pocket could either wash those smelly clothes or buy his dinner. He'd picked dinner.

"Miss Jackie is one of the few citizens of this town that gives a darn about us homeless people," he answered.

"You don't need pity," Bill growled. You need a job.

Harry's voice trembled, "You think I haven't tried to get work. Two years ago, I looked just like you, Mr. Executive. It doesn't take long to reach this state. You should know that. All you need is the couple of drinks, you've been yelling about all night."

Jackie timidly intervened. "He's right. I've been sitting here all evening envisioning a similar future because I just lost my job today."

"Oh really, Miss Efficiency, chimed in Angie. Is that why you were looking your superior nose down at me all night? Did you really think I didn't see you?"

"Anyone can have bad luck and lose a job, but there is no excuse for that outfit you're wearing or your occupation" replied Jackie.

"Well, Miss Priss, you tell me what occupation you select when your forced to get a job at fourteen years of age," snapped Angie.

Santa Claus who had been trying to disappear into his seat suddenly leaned forward. Angie got her first full look at him. She leaped from her seat, stumbling clumsily in her heels, and fell full length into his lap.

"Mark, oh Mark. You finally came," she kept murmuring.

"My sweet Angel, what's happened to you?" Mark whispered. "I knew it was you when I heard your voice, but I never would have recognized you.

Angie recoiled, "I'm so ashamed, Mark for you to see me like this. I was so hungry. I didn't know what else to do. The little money I'd saved was stolen from me before I even got out of the bus station. Then this man approached me. I thought he looked decent. He told me he could help me make a lot of money. Once I was in his hotel, he made me too afraid to leave. He hid my clothes and gave me this outfit to wear. I had no money. I had no home. So, I did what he asked." Angie lifted her tearstained face and stared at her brother.

"Oh please Mark, don't hate me. Tonight, I finally found the courage to leave him. I had no idea what to do next, so I came in here to dry off and think.

Mark was sobbing too. "Don't worry Angel. It's all over now. None of it was your fault. It was mine for not coming you in time. God sent me here in here tonight. I'd planned to leave tomorrow. But you're safe now, Angel. Your safe with me."

The other three occupants at the table were stunned into silence. At that moment the waitress appeared carrying food.

"I see you've all gotten acquainted," she said as she set down a huge plate of steaming rice and a plate of sweet and sour chicken. Then the other waitress arrived an enormous plate of broccoli, snow peas, and water chestnuts.

"This best I can do with no electric," she said. "I hope you all enjoy meal very much." Then she bowed elegantly and glided away. Four of the diners sat staring wordlessly at the food, but Harry immediately piled chicken and rice and broccoli onto his plate.

This is all very touching," he said, "but I haven't eaten in two days."

Hungrily he crunched on broccoli and water chestnuts. Angel and Mark had moved their chairs closer together and were sniffing and whispering every couple of seconds. Bill finally moved to fill his plate, all the while watching Jackie. She looked amazingly like his ex-wife, but she seemed much more vulnerable. Even now she was fighting back tears of remorse. She'd been so cruel to Angie, judging her and not even knowing her story.

Bill ladled some food onto her plate. "It's all right. I know how you feel. I misjudged poor Harry here too. He's absolutely right. A couple of drinks and I'd be in worse shape than he is, but I'd have no excuse."

Jackie reached her hand across the table and grasped Angie's hand.

"I'm sorry, Angie," she said. "I am a Priss. What I said to you was inexcusable. I didn't even know your circumstances."

Angie squeezed her hand and smiled. Even through the thick layers of makeup, she looked years younger. "It's all right," she declared. "I can forgive anything today. Besides I wasn't very nice to Harry either. He can't help his situation. Forgive me please, Harry." Then she faced Mark.

"Um, Mark, I have to go to the ladies room. I'll be right back." She wobbled off to the bathroom taking careful steps in the dark. Jackie tasted her food then and realizing how hungry she was eating ravenously. Mark sat beaming. He put a couple spoonful on his plate as everyone watched, but he never touched it the rest of the evening. Then he loaded Angel's plate looking as anxious as a proud father. Bill was the last one to eat. Then he ate slowly never taking his eyes off Jackie. After a few minutes, he put his fork down.

"Jackie," he said, "I know we just met tonight, but I have a huge empty house that I rattle around in over on the East Side. I would be pleased if you join me for Christmas Dinner tomorrow unless you have other plans."

"No Bill, my plans were a TV dinner and a rented movie, but if it's all right with you, I have an even better idea. Then she leaned over and whispered something in his ear.

Harry surveyed the table. Everyone seemed to be finished with their meal except Angel who hadn't returned yet. He faced Bill, Uh, do you think I could eat the rest. We don't want it to go to waste," he said smiling sheepishly.

Jackie looked on sympathetically "Take it Harry, we've all eaten. And I don't think Angie's worried much about food."

At that moment Angel came striding back. She had washed all the make up off and braided her hair in two long braids. She had even broken the heels off her shoes. She now looked about ten. She sat down and in between hugs from Mark, ate her dinner. When everyone was completely finished, Jackie and Bill who had whispered together for the last ten minutes both smiled and Bill stood up.

"Harry," he said. "I want to offer you a job in my company. It's not much, but it's a start. You just have to show up Monday morning at my office nine o clock sharp clean and ready to work.

"Oh My God", whispered Harry. "Do you really mean it? You're actually going to give me a chance? Oh, thank you, thank you." He grasped Bills hand and pumped it vigorously.

"Now for the other news," Bill said, "You're all invited tomorrow for Christmas Dinner at my home.

Angie smiled sadly. "I'd love to come but all I have are the clothes on my back and I'm going to burn these as soon as I'm humanly able to."

Harry plucked at his ragged coat. "I guess I'm in that category too. I'd like to toss these rags in the river, but I've nothing else to wear."

Suddenly Mark grabbed the Santa Claus beard and put it on. Then with a big smile, he said. Both of them will be there, Bill. Let Santa Claus handle it."

Jackie laughed and clapped her hands together. "You know I thought this would be the worst night of my life, but I've never been happier. I feel that we five people who have met here tonight will be friends forever."

And you and I are going to be extra special friends," declared Bill.

At that moment, the lights flickered twice and went on. A young waitress approached.

"Hi," she said. "I've brought you your fortune cookies. Did you all enjoy your dinner? By the way there's no charge. We never charge on Christmas Eve."

Harry said excitedly, "the food was terrific, just terrific, but where is the waitress, the one with those tiny, little feet? The one that made us all sit at this table?"

The waitress looked confused. It's just my sister and I. My father cooked the food. There is no one else.

Jackie interjected, "But she was so nice. We all saw her. We wanted to thank her for what she's done for us tonight."

Mark called excitedly, "Jackie, open your fortune cookie. See what yours says."

In the silence that followed, Bill said. "Well, I'll be—They all say the same thing and then he read HE WHO BEFRIENDS A LOST SOUL REAPS THE GOODNESS OF MANKIND."

"Maybe that little waitress wasn't a waitress after all," mused Angie.

"I'm just about certain she wasn't," said Mark.

"Well, whoever she was, she made it a Merry Christmas for us," said Harry.

"She certainly did," Bill said hugging Jackie.

"The best Christmas ever," agreed Jackie.

BECCA'S GOLDEN KEY

BECCA'S GOLDEN KEY

ONCE UPON A time there lived a beautiful little girl with two golden brown ponytails and big brown eyes in a cute little cottage in the woods. She lived there with her mommy and daddy, and they were all very happy. Some days they would go fishing in the brook behind the house. One day Becca caught five fish and mommy cooked them for dinner. Other days they walked to the lake at the edge of the forest and swim half the day, then have a picnic later on a blanket in the sun, eating Becca's favorite, grape juice and peanut butter and jelly sandwiches.

One day when they were walking in the woods, Becca saw a beautiful white rabbit. She went chasing after it.

"Becca, Becca," mommy called, "come back," but Becca kept going. She wanted that rabbit.

Suddenly the sun disappeared behind a cloud and on the tree above them a hideous old witch appeared.

"Where is the little one?" she cackled. "I want her."

Marcus looked worriedly up the path He didn't want Becca to return now.

"Oh don't worry," said the old witch. "You must give me your permission or else I can't take her, but I can teach her all my magic powers. She will make a great sorceress."

"Go away old witch," said Kate, the girl's mother. "You will not take our daughter."

The old witch remained on the branch grumbling and muttering until Marcus picked up one of the hard green apples that littered the ground and threw it at the old witch with all his might. It hit her right between the eyes, and she fell with a mighty crash.

"You will pay for that," she shrieked as she got up. "The next time you see your beloved daughter she will be as old as you.

Then she took her crooked wand and wave it. The parents found themselves back in the cottage. The old witch went straight to the old grandfather clock and stole the golden key. Then she waved her wand again and the clock stopped ticking, the pendulum stopped swinging. The parents stopped moving. They fell asleep in their tracks. Even the birds stopped singing around the cottage.

"There" said the old witch, "I have stopped time here and unless someone finds this golden key and restarts the clock, they will not wake up for 50 years."

Then she gave a horrible screech and disappeared in a cloud of black smoke.

Now the trick was the golden key that the old witch stole from the grandfather clock would start everything up again so she had to hide it and hide it well. She flew through the forest on her broom trying to decide where to hide the old key. Then she spotted the lake. Fish were leaping up to catch the flies that buzzed overhead. One leaped up just as she tossed the key. He swallowed it whole.

"Now," she said as she flew away, "let them find the key now."

Meanwhile little Becca had finally caught the white rabbit. She kissed him on his cute little head and walked back carrying him to the spot where she'd left her parents. They weren't there. Little Becca started to cry. The rabbit wriggled to the ground. When his feet touched the ground, he turned into a little man. A leprechaun.

"My name is lucky," he said. "The old witch turned me into a bunny when I wouldn't show her where my gold was. Now, Honey, the old witch has already cast a spell on your parents but we'll go see anyway."

When they reached the cottage, everything was still. Nothing moved. Even the butterflies which flew constantly around the rosebush sat motionless on the flowers. Inside, her parents lay sound asleep. Lucky looked at the clock.

Looks like she stopped time. Do you have a key to the clock?" asked Lucky.

Becca, who'd been trying to wake her mommy jumped up.

"We have a golden key," she said. "A beautiful golden key."

"Well, the old witch has it. She can't take mortal things back to her kingdom, but she has probably hidden it in the woods. The animals will help us find it. Come on, Becca, we'll find the key."

"But mommy and daddy won't wake up."

"They will, little Becca soon as we find the key."

Back at the lake mother bear was fishing for her cubs. She caught them back to her cave and whacked them hard so they'd stop jumping. The golden key flew out the fish's mouth and landed on the cave floor.

That's pretty mom," little cub Brian said. "That golden key."

"Yes," said little cub Suzy, can we play with it."

"Sure," said mom, "after you have your supper."

The little bears played with the key until their daddy came home. Then they left it on the path trying to beat daddy home. A raccoon came along and thought it would make a shiny addition his collection and took it home to his den.

Becca and Lucky started on their journey to find the golden key. They walked a long way into the woods and Becca got very tired and hungry. Lucky did some magic and soon produced a peanut butter and jelly sandwich and a tall glass of cold milk. After Becca ate, she felt much better but she was still very tired so Lucky went looking to find her a safe place to sleep. Not far from where they sat was the bear's cave. So Lucky went to the cave and asked, "can little Becca sleep here tonight. We're far from home."

"Of course," said the mommy bear, "come in Becca."

After Becca came into the cave, the first thing she said was, "did any of you see my golden key? It's very important."

The little bears looked at each other.

"We were playing with a golden key," said Bryan.

"It fell out of mommy's fish," said Suzy.

"We left it on the path, when you came in our cave you would see it," the cubs said.

"Oh, no," said Becca sadly but she was so tired she fell asleep immediately snuggled between the two furry cubs.

The next day Lucky and Becca spotted Mr. Raccoon.

"Did you see my golden key?" asked Becca.

"Why, yes," said the raccoon. "I was adding it to my collection when this huge old eagle swooped down and grabbed it. You'll have to ask Mr. Eagle."

They walked a little farther and there was Mr. Eagle trying to pull a worm from the ground.

"Have you seen my golden key?" Mr. Eagle asked Becca.

"Sure did, little lady. I thought it was some new kind of food, but it was hard and not very tasty. I dropped it but I saw Mr. Squirrel grab it.

They walked a little farther and there was Mr. Squirrel trying to fit more acorns into his tree hole.

"Mr. Squirrel, have you seen my golden key? asked Becca.

"I tried to stuff it in my tree but it wouldn't fit," said Mr. Squirrel. It fell out right on to Mr. Turtle's back.

Lucky could see Becca was getting tired again. He hoped they'd find the key soon. Mr. Turtle had encountered Miss Deer who loved to play near Becca's cottage. Soon as she saw the key, she said "that's Becca's golden key. I will take it home to her."

When she reached the cottage, it seemed as though no one was there so Miss Deer dropped the key in Becca's mailbox and then stood there uncertainly. It was so quiet. Too quiet.

Lucky and Becca walked so far, they were almost home again when Becca saw Mr. Turtle.

"Mr. Turtle, have you seen my golden key. asked Becca.

Mr. Turtle looked up slowly. "Why, Becca, Miss Deer just took that key. She said she was giving it to you."

Becca and Lucky ran to the cottage. They got there just as Miss Deer was leaving.

Oh, Becca, there you are," she said. I put your golden key in the mailbox. I knew it was yours, but something is wrong here. It's way too quiet."

"We know," said Lucky. "We just need the key to fix everything.'

Lucky lifted her up and Becca grabbed the key. Then they ran in the house. Weeds were already growing around the door. When Becca reached the grandfather clock, she turned the key once and the birds started singing again. She turned it twice and the butterflies flitted again from flower to flower but when Becca turned it the third time, her parents woke up and hugged their little girl.

We're so glad you're alright, Honey, and you broke the old witch's curse. Thank you, thank you."

"Now that you, all together again, I guess I'll be going," said Lucky. "I left you a little present on the shelf over there. If it weren't for Becca, I'd still be a rabbit. Then he vanished in a puff of green smoke.

They all ran to the shelf and looked. There sat a huge pot of gold coins, enough to last two lifetimes. Beside it was a note. I have put a spell on your house, so the old witch can never come near you again and the gold coins are a present. Thanks again, Lucky.

Mommy and Daddy and little Becca were very happy. They all hugged each other again and they all lived happily ever after.

"FIRE"

A TALL DARK figure watched angrily as those people moved into his house. For two years the house had remained empty, ever since he'd chased the last intruders out. Now someone else was moving in.

He could hear their voices pitched high in excitement directing the furniture movers where to place each piece of furniture. Then he saw her—A little girl. Dainty and tiny she was, with a beautiful smile. Though they were a few blocks up the street, he could see her perfectly. Her soft reddish-brown hair and big dark eyes, and her enormous dimples as she clung to her Daddy's hand.

So much like his own daughter who'd died two hundred years ago. No matter, he thought, they're not going to live in my house.

The young wife Anna, who'd been checking out the neighborhood saw the dark, grotesque figure standing only a few blocks away. She tugged on her husband's sleeve.

"Honey," She whispered. "Look, who's that?"

But when they both turned to look again, the figure was gone.

"Must've been a trick of the light," he said with a smile, and went on directing the placement of a beautiful grandfather clock, they'd just purchased. Anna wasn't sure about that. She kept glancing at the spot where she'd seen the figure and little chills chased themselves up and down her back, as she realized that particular spot was the neighborhood cemetery.

The menacing figure was forgotten in the next few weeks as they arranged furniture, put up pictures and curtains. Only one room needed to be painted. Everything else was in perfect shape. The house was beautiful. All the floors were carpeted and rich pine colored wood lined all the baseboards and banisters in the house. They couldn't believe their luck.

One evening about a month after Anna and Edward had settled in, they sat discussing the day's events in the family room. The baby monitor was set up so they could hear Elizabeth as soon as she woke.

And then they did hear Elizabeth, but she wasn't crying. She was giggling and talking her baby talk, which was a series of babble interspersed with Ma Ma and Da Da.

"Who is she talking to? asked Edward

Alarmed Anna ran to Elizabeth's bedroom. Little Elizabeth standing in the crib chirping away happily, but there was no one else in the room. She noticed a slight movement of the rocking chair, but dismissed that as a slight breeze from the window. Lifting Elizabeth from her crib, she changed her quickly and took her downstairs to join Daddy.

The next day Anna took Elizabeth for a walk around the entire block. All the houses were painted a different color, some with quaint old lamp posts in the front. Every house looked picture book perfect. The ideal neighborhood. Then she came to the end of the block.

There sat the cemetery. An old weather-beaten sign professed it to be The Elm Street Cemetery. Cautiously Anna stepped in between the rusted iron gates which hung open. She pushed Elizabeth's stroller carefully between the gravestones, reading the names. Most of the stones were dated 1845 or later. She moved cautiously along reading the stones when suddenly she stopped in shock.

The stone directly in front of her read Samuel Taylor, died 1800, but scratched on the top in large, uneven letters, was the word COLORED. Anna looked around. From this spot, she could see right up her street and directly at her own house. This is where the figure she'd seen had been standing. She grasped the stroller and practically ran to the front gate. Could it be possible she'd been a ghost? Anna hurried into the house and locked the doors, and all the windows. Even then she continued shaking long after Elizabeth was asleep. When Edward came home, Anna told him what she'd seen today in trembling tones.

"Oh, Honey, now you've gone and upset yourself over nothing. You said yourself those old gates are always open. Any tramp strolling by could've decided that was a good, quiet place to spend the night. That he was standing there watching us, would that be so usual? Maybe he was thinking of asking us for a handout."

"Sweetheart, he looked so ominous though. He didn't look friendly.

"Really, Anna, you could barely see him. How could you surmise all that? I, myself, never saw him at all."

Anna said nothing more, but she had a bad feeling about this, and her feelings never lied.

As the weeks passed by, other strange things happened in the Johnson household. Anna looked for a favorite mixing bowl knowing already it wouldn't be there. Later when she'd given up trying to find it, Edward would look in the exact same cupboard and there it sat. Anna wondered if she was losing her mind, because it happened again and again in the next several days. Finally, one evening she looked for her salad bowl. It was not in its usual place. Very quietly she went and got Edward. They tiptoed into the kitchen. She pointed to the empty closet.

"Look," she whispered. "No salad bowl."

He nodded.

"Come with me."

In the other room, they sat without saying a word for ten minutes. Now she motioned for Edward to follow her back to the kitchen, which he did. She opened the same closet.

"Look," she shouted.

Edward gasped. There sat the bowl in its usual place. Then he knew Anna wasn't just being forgetful. Something else was happening that couldn't be explained away so easily. Something very mysterious.

Other strange things started to happen too. Though they listened to Elizabeth's monitor every night, they never heard her talking again, yet when she played in the family room, they noticed names she'd repeat when playing with her dolls. Names they never heard before, like Samuel and Bessie and once they even swore they heard her say fireplace. There were no children in her Day Care with those names. They made a point of checking.

One evening Samuel stood by the outside door to the basement watching the Johnson family. Edward was reading a book to Elizabeth and as he reached the end of each page, little Elizabeth would smile and turn the page. The light from the stove lit the color of her hair to a fiery red and highlighted her brilliant smile and dimpled cheeks. Anna sat in the huge chair sipping her coffee, but her eyes were on Elizabeth and Edward.

Samuel had loved his family exclusively. He understood the admiration and adoration that shone in her eyes. It confused him. Edward and the child were his color, but Anna was Caucasian. In his day, it was her very people who'd burned him and his family to death.

"Honey, do you feel a draft?" Edward interrupted his reading to say. "It seems to be coming from the cellar door.

They both looked in that direction. A pale white mist shimmered in front of the door. As they both watched, it turned into a stream of fog and floated gently through the door. "That was him! Anna shouted dropping her coffee.

"Him? him who?" Edward asked holding Elizabeth closer.

"It was Samuel! The ghost! I know it was. He's been toying with us for weeks." Anna hugged Elizabeth and Edward with shaking hands.

Edward pulled his wife closer. "Are you saying, Honey, you want to move? After all," he said with a smile, "This is Massachusetts. All these old houses have a ghost or two and ours has been relatively harmless up to now."

Anna whispered, "he talks to the baby. We don't know what he's teaching her."?

Edward looked down at the child. "That's true," he said. I'll start looking for a place for us to move to tomorrow, and see if there's any chance of getting back any compensation for anything that we've invested in the house. Think you can stick it out for a few more days?"

Anna looked at their beautiful home.

"Yes, I think I can," she said as her eyes filled with tears.

The next day, Anna got off early. Instead of picking up Elizabeth right away, she went to the local library to read old newspapers. After searching through stacks of newspapers, Anna went to the room where the ancient newspapers were on microfilm. She found what she was looking for immediately.

The headline read January 10, 1800, Samuel Taylor, wife Edna and daughter Bessie were burned to death in their home on 920 Elm Street by a fire of questionable origin. Neighbors buried the family in The Elm Street Cemetery usually reserved only for whites as the Taylor family lived and served on Elm Street all their lives.

Anna dropped the spindle and the microfiche film went flying back by itself, whirling and snapping, almost flying off the roll. A few others in the room sent annoyed looks het way. Anna got up shakily. No wonder, she thought. Samuel and his whole family burned to death. No wonder he haunted the house. She picked up Elizabeth and drove home nervously.

The house was quiet. No sounds except for the ticking of the clocks and the soft rumble when the furnace turned on, but Anna sensed Samuel's presence.

"Samuel," she whispered. "I know the secret. I understand your rage. But why do you haunt us? We love your house as much as you did, and we know you love the baby. You speak to her all the time.

Only silence answered her plea. Anna fed Elizabeth and then gave her some Cheerios for a snack. She put the baby in the play area with her toys and returned to the kitchen to wash the dishes. The Cheerios box shed left on the table was completely empty. Spelled out on the kitchen table, the Cheerios arranged in neat letters, were the words, THE HOUSE WAS DEEDED TO ME BY MY OWNER AND MY WIFE AND I WERE FREE THAT IS WHAT YOU DO NOT KNOW THE FAMILY OF MY PREVIOUS OWNER KILLED US TO GET THE HOUSE.

Anna stared. "We didn't do it." Anna yelled. "We love the house. Please let us live here." But she no longer sensed him in the house.

He had gone. Anna left the display of Cheerios so Edward could see it when he returned. Then though it was damp and chilly out, she bundled up Elizabeth and took her out for a walk to visit one of their neighbors. Anna picked the oldest couple on the block, Sadie and Tom Jacobson who'd lived on Elm Street all their lives.

Sadie answered the door. "Why Mrs. Johnson, we were wondaing when you'd hona us with a visit. Come on in. What a cute young un you have there. Sit down and I'll get out the tea and scones."

After they were comfortably settled and Elizabeth playing with some blocks on the floor, "Mrs. Jacobson," said Anna. "I'd like to ask you a couple questions about the house we live in."

"Uh Oh," said Sadie. "I knew this was coming soon. Some strange things happening over there, huh?"

"Yes," answered Anna with a smile. "A few."

"Well, I'll tell you, Mrs. Johnson."

"Anna, please."

"Well, Anna we've lived on this street for fifty years and we've seen, old Tom and I two of the strangest fires ever. A young couple, just like yourselves, came screaming out in the snow one January night, and Lawd knows I looked myself. Their whole house was a blazing inferno. They were rushed to a hotel to spend the night and all the fire trucks in Sudbury came a rushing out to put the fire out and then

Anna whispered, "then what, Sadie?

Then we all looked at that house and there wasn't a spark on it." "What?" Anna gasped. "What do you mean?"

"The house wasn't burnt at all. We'd all seen it burning, but the house was untouched. And you know what? That wasn't the strangest thing. It happened again. Another family moved in. A big family and sure thing, that January, in the middle of a snowstorm, they all came a running out, and the house ablazing again. Ten minutes later, there sat the house without a spark on it. The fire company thought we neighbors were playing pranks on em, but I promise you, Anna, and everyone on this street can verify, that house was on fire."

"Sadie, I certainly do believe you and I thank you for being so candid with me."

She looked at Elizabeth, who was falling asleep on the floor.

"I think I'd better get the baby home now for her nap, but I thank you again and those scones were delicious."

"Come over anytime and get the recipe and you know what, I don't think you people will have any trouble over there. You're such a nice couple. Maybe you broke the curse."

"I hope so, and thanks again," called Anna, as she carried Elizabeth back home.

Samuel watched silently from the living room as the family ate their supper. It was getting close to the anniversary of his death and time for him to get rid of them for good, but for weeks now, he'd done nothing to scare them.

Anna had decided to remain in the house since all supernatural activity had ceased since the Cheerios incident. Anna decided her plea to Samuel had touched his heart and he'd decided to let them live in the house in peace. Edward, though was not so sure. He called his mother in Pennsylvania for advice. After he'd told her the whole story, there was silence at the other end.

"Mom?"

Yes, Edward, I was just thinking. You say Anna seems to have a special telepathy whenever he's around? Maybe she should talk to him. Just explain things to him like she did when he arranged the Cheerios".

Mom, this is no flesh and blood man. It's a ghost! I told her and now I tell you, you can't reason with a ghost"

"Oh, Honey, all your life, you've always seen everything in shades of either black or white. There are many shades of gray in between. How do you know what can't be done until you try it?" 'There are many things in heaven and earth, Edward than are dreamt of in your philosophy'

"Mom, what about the baby? He talks to her all the time."

"Yes, and from what you've told me, she shows no sign of fear of him. Babies are very perceptive. They haven't yet lost the wonder of life. Look, I love the three of you and I don't want any harm to come to any of you. If bad things keep happening, get out immediately, but let Anna talk to him.

I think he's a lost soul who needs advice to show him where to go".

O.K., I hope you're right, Goodbye Mom".

Goodbye, Honey, and stay safe."

Samuel still talked to the little girl, and he'd fallen in love with her. Her cheerful smile reminded him of his own little one and how much he missed her. Now, as he watched them at dinner, laughing and enjoying each other's company, he realized he didn't want to chase them away. His house held the light of love again, as it had when he himself lived there. He realized when they were gone, it would be just a cold empty house again.

Another thing that surprised him was Anna. She spoke to him all the time. She seemed to know always when he was near even though he left no betraying signs such as the mist they'd seen that one time. Just yesterday she'd been making the beds, and looked directly where he sat in the chair by the window, and said "you know, Samuel, I know how angry you are at the family that destroyed your family but it was part of the same family that gave you the house in the first place. They must've loved you very much."

Samuel had never thought of that. It was true. He'd loved his old master who'd always treated him with dignity. Strange too that out of all the families that had lived in this house, no one ever knew when he was near. They'd been frightened by the things he did, but they didn't see him as Elizabeth did. She smiled and stood in her crib the second he entered her room. He adored the little one most of all. He'd often make little things float around her room so he could watch her giggle in delight.

Even now as they ate their dinner, Anna would glance his way occasionally and Elizabeth grinned at him happily through spaghetti covered lips. No, Samuel decided, I don't want this family to go.

Christmas came and went. The old house glowed with the twinkling lights and spirit of love. Samuel watched Elizabeth play with the pile of toys she received for Christmas in the family room.

Watching this family react with such love and devotion to each other was causing Samuel to miss his own family more and more, but he no longer knew how to reach them.

January 10th arrived. D-Day! as in Destroy, but Samuel had long ago decided to leave this family alone. Now he watched silently as Edward loaded the stove with wood in the family room. Outside the huge picture window snow fell gently, smacking wet little kisses against the glass. The tree lights twinkled sending little sparkles of light on the snow that drifted against the window sill. Edward shoved another log in and slammed the door shut, unaware that it didn't completely close.

"Honey, could you come up here and help me a minute?", Anna called.

She was preparing a snack they could eat by the fire.

"Now, Bethy, you stay away from that stove and Mommy and Daddy will be right back with good things to eat.

"O.K., Da Da", Elizabeth called back.

In the kitchen Anna was preparing sandwiches and snacks, and a tray of vegetables. She needed Edward to open a bottle of wine.

Down in the basement, the huge log Edward had placed in the stove caught fire and blazed away shooting sparks out the few inches the door was left open. Most of the sparks landed on the bricks surrounding the stove, but a few fell on the nearby rug and were now smoking.

Upstairs the ventilator system was running, dispensing any smoke from the stove, so the smoking carpet was not immediately detected. Samuel watched in alarm as the smoldering carpet suddenly burst into flames, and neither Anna nor Edward returned for the baby.

Suddenly Anna did get a good whiff of smoke, but when Edward turned to run down the steps, she grasped his hand.

"It's not real", she said. "It's Samuel. I know it. It's January 10th. He's trying to scare us out with a fake fire."

"It smells pretty real to me", said Edward.

That's the point", said Anna. "He wants us to run, but we won't. This time he won't scare this family away."

In the basement, sparks were bursting into flames all around the stove and Elizabeth stood at the bottom of the steps screaming in fear. When Edward heard the baby cries, he knew this was no fake fire. He shoved Anna out the side porch door and raced to the steps to rescue Elizabeth. Aw o smoke exploded into his face forcing him back, though he kept struggling down the steps until the acrid smell caused him to black out and tumble halfway down the steps.

In the basement, Samuel grabbed the child who was coughing helplessly now and took her out the back door. He sat her on a little porch out of reach of the wet snow and even threw an old blanket out there drying, over her. It was only then he realized he'd been physically able to lift the child and feel her warm body next to his though he was only a spirit. If he could save the child, maybe he could save the father too. He returned to the flame filled room.

Anna, who was on the porch, knew now this was no fake fire and she was screaming for her family. No one came out and she could see flames through the basement window where just minutes ago her baby was playing. She fell to the porch crying and screaming for help. Then she saw a strange sight.

Down the huge snow-covered hill behind the house, she could see huge mounds of snow moving towards the back of their house and into the house. Then over the hissing sound of the steam as the snow put out the fire, she could hear Elizabeth crying. She ran down the back steps slipping on the hard grey patches of frozen snow. On the back porch sat the baby crying, wrapped in an old moth-eaten blanket. But where was Edward?

Even as she stood there another mound of snow moved by itself up the hillside and into the house and put out the sparks still smoldering on the carpet. Then through the open door came Edward floating four feet in the air. Anna gasped. Gently, he was laid down next to her. It was only then that Anna realized he was unconscious.

"Honey, Honey, wake up", she yelled, as she rubbed snow on his face and frantically shook him until finally he coughed a few times and opened his eyes.

"The baby, get the baby", he yelled, trying to get up.

"She's right here, Darling. Just rest. Samuel saved her and you too. He even put out the fire. The real fire!

Up the street came three screaming fire engines, and soon the firemen were roaming the basement checking to see if all the flames were out. Finally, the Chief came out where they still sat on the porch shivering.

"Everything's out", he said. "Only thing destroyed is the rug and a few toys. We'll take that out. Quick thinking using the snow to put out the fire. Don't know how just the two of you did it. Quite amazing. Sorry about being so slow in coming. This house has a bad reputation for false alarms. You should be able to go back in soon. Smoke's clearing out pretty fast."

Now some of the neighbors appeared to help. Sadie carried several blankets.

"Wrap this around you and come over my house until that smoke clears out. Guess I was wrong about old Samuel after all, she said.

"No", Anna whispered. "You were right. He saved our baby and Edward. He even put out the fire. I guess he's going to let us stay.

Slowly they climbed the icy steps to reach the front of the house. Anna looked immediately to the cemetery. There he stood, but no longer in darkness. There was a brilliant white light around him and when he saw they were watching, he made a low bow and tipped his hat, and over the sound of the wind and the whirling snow, they all clearly heard him say,

"Going home to see my family. Take good care of my house now and especially take care of that little Darling".

Then the brilliant light and Samuel simply vanished.

The End

EMERGENCY

LITTLE BENNY LOVED to drive. He was only eight years old but all he could think of was driving. He'd take the cars that Daddy bought him and line them up on the sidewalk like a real highway. Then he'd drive his car around the others pretending to be a real driver. Sometimes he'd get the other kids to play with him, but they were no fun. They just wanted to crash the cars together and laugh. Little Benny really wanted to drive.

Whenever he went shopping with his Mom, he'd watch carefully when she started the car, the way she clicked the turn signals when she wanted to turn, even how she used the brake. He really wanted to drive.

One day Benny's mother took him to visit one of her friends, Barbara. Barbara had two little boys, so Benny and her two boys played outside while the mothers sat inside and talked.

Dan, Billy, and Benny played for a while with Billy's fire engine Tonka truck. Then Benny noticed Mommy had parked her car just down the street from her friend's house.

"I can really drive, you know," he told Dan. "I watch Mommy all the time."

"Oh, you cannot" yelled Billy. "Your too small."

"I can too." Benny peeped at his mom. She and Barbara were watching the Oprah show and talking.

"I'll prove it," Benny said. "Get in my mom's car and I'll take you for a ride."

Billy and Dan hurried to hop in the car and Benny hopped in the driver's seat

"Ha, ha," Billy laughed. We can't go anywhere. Your Mom took the keys."

Benny sat up in the seat. He turned the steering wheel and made driving noises. Other children were gathering now on the sidewalk watching Benny pretend to drive. Billy waved his hand out the window.

"Good-bye," he called. "We're going on a trip."

Then Benny did something awful. He reached down and unlatched the emergency brake. The car which sat on an incline went careening down the hill The children watching scattered away, but one little girl almost got struck by the car before it crashed to a halt on someone's uninhabited stoop.

The frightened children all ran away even as Dan and Billy jumped quickly out of the car. Only Benny still sat in the driver's seat shaking and crying. He'd almost hit that little girl. Barbara and his mom, Megan came running out of the house.

"Benny, what's wrong with you?" shouted his mother. You almost hit | that little girl.'."

She reached into the car and yanked on the brake.

"Go sit with Barbara," she told Benny. "I'll have to see what damage has been done.'

She climbed in carefully, protecting her eight-month pregnant belly. Then slowly she released the brake, put the car in reverse and backed slowly up the hill. One fender was damaged, but the stoop he'd hit remained unbroken and the house was unoccupied.

Now with the car parked again, on trembling legs she told Barbara, I think we need to go home. Benny needs to think about what he almost did in his room, and I'm a wreck. I'm going to lay down too."

Barbara smiled sympathetically. "I understand. Now you call me if you have any problems. You have to take care of yourself in your condition.

All the way home there was silence except for the slight squeak, they could hear every time the fender brushed against the wheel. When they reached the house, Mom took a pair of pliers from the glove compartment and pushed at the dent until the fender was off the tire.

There, she said tiredly. "That will have to do until we can have it fixed. Now you go to your room and think about what could have happened today, and ^never try to drive that car again. I'm going to lay down for a while too."

She looked at his woebegone face and gave him a big hug.

"I know you didn't mean any harm, Honey, but I really need to rest my nerves right now. We'll talk about this later."

Sometime later Benny woke up. He'd fallen asleep and mom hadn't come. She'd never punish him this long. On wobbly legs, he ran to her room. Mom was asleep but she was moaning and holding her belly as she twisted from side to side.

"Mom, Mom, wake up!" Benny shouted, "Are you all right?"

Megan opened her eyes and then grimaced, "Oh, Benny, I think the babies coming. I'm going to need your help. Barbara's too far away. Call 911. I don t think we have much time.'

Benny hurried to dial the phone.

Mom, he called frantically. "I keep getting a busy signal."

A busy signal. Megan gasped. "That can't be. They never have a busy signal. How will I get to the hospital?"

Benny ran to the window. Their neighbors on both sides were on vacation. The people across the street were at work, Daddy was out of town. There was no one to ask. Then he spotted the car still sitting in the driveway.

His Mom had the same thought. "Come, Benny," she whispered. "I'm going to have to try to drive myself."

Benny grabbed the suitcase already packed in the hall closet and threw it in the trunk. Then he tried to help his mom to the car. Every few steps, she'd bend down clutching her stomach and groaning.

When they reached the car, Benny said, "Mom, you can't drive like that, but I can. I know you told me never to touch the car again, but this is an emergency and Mom, I really can drive."

"NO, Benny, You can't. Oh, oh," she whispered, "I think my water just broke. I have to lay down."

Benny helped his mother into the back seat. "Just lay down, Mom. I can do it. It will be O.K."

Once his mom was in the car. Benny climbed in the driver's seat. He took a deep breath. He was really scared. First, he fastened his seat belt, then turned on the ignition. He released the brake and very slowly put his foot on the gas. He had to really stretch to reach the gas and brake pedals, but he could do it. Now, he had to turn left onto Johnson Street. Lots of traffic, but Benny knew what to do. He pulled into the middle lane and speeded up.

He could hear his mother gasping in the back seat. He had to hurry. He turned right on to Ninth Street, just a few more blocks to go. Then suddenly just ahead, there it was Memorial Hospital. He pulled in behind an ambulance and even remembered to pull on the emergency brakes.

Then he ran in the door screaming, "My Mom needs help'. Please Come! Hurry!"

One of the nurses pushed a little buzzer and suddenly there were two men in white coats carrying a stretcher for his mother. As they carried her off, she grasped his hand for a moment.

"Thank you, Benny," she whispered. "My brave little boy."

The nurse led Benny to a room where he could sit down. A white hair and a camera approached Benny.

"I hear you're a hero," he said.

Benny just looked confused.

"The 911 lines were all down because of a storm over in Pittston" said the man, "but we heard you got your Mommy to the hospital all on your own."

Then they took Benny's picture and wrote some stuff down and went away. Just then the nurse returned, and she was smiling.

"You can come in and see your mother, now," she said.

His Mom looked very tired, but in her arms was the most beautiful baby he'd ever seen.

"Come meet your new baby sister," she said. We're both here alive and well because of you, Honey, so what do you think we should name her.?"

I think, said Benny, giving his mother a big hug. "We should call her Miracle."

THE HARDEST JOB OF ALL

"JOSH WAKE UP! School Today!" Josh's mother called from the kitchen downstairs. Josh sat up and yawned just as his mom came into his room carrying his baby sister Betsy.

"Hurry Josh!" she said, "or you won't have time for breakfast.

She set baby Betsy down and began laying out all his clothes for school, while Josh washed his face and brushed his teeth.

"Guess what, Mom?" he called from the bathroom.

"What, Honey?" answered mom, as she put clean underwear on the pile.

"Today I'm going to find out who has the hardest job of all."

"Why that's wonderful, Honey. Let me know what you find out," Then she scooped up Betsy and went to change her diaper. Breakfast is on the table, she called over her shoulder. Mom leaned down just as Josh flew out into the hallway, and planted a big kiss on his forehead.

"Have a great day at school," she called.

The first person Josh met on the way to school was Mr. Jackson, the policeman, who always helped him cross the street. When he was safely on the other side of the street, he asked Mr. Jackson, "is your job the hardest job of all?"

He watched the traffic going up and down the street.

"It looks pretty hard," Josh said.

Mr. Jackson said, "I do have to direct all the traffic and make sure all the drivers follow the rules. Sometimes I even have to catch robbers and take them to jail. But I wouldn't say it was the hardest job of all."

Thanks, Mr. Jackson. I'll keep looking," said Josh and he continued to school.

When Josh reached school and went to his room, Mrs. Johnson was writing rows and rows of numbers on the blackboard.

"Mrs. Johnson?" Josh asked. "You have to teach all the children in my class. Is that the hardest job of all?"

Mrs. Johnson stopped writing and smiled.

"Some children need a lot of teaching. I have to show them how to do their math problems, and help them with their reading, and teach them science, but I wouldn't say it was the hardest job of all."

"Thank you, Mrs. Johnson," said Josh. "I guess I have to keep looking."

Josh worked on his lessons until eleven thirty. At eleven thirty the bell rang for playground time. So, all the children ran out to the playground. Josh was having great fun playing baseball until he grabbed the bat and caught a splinter in his finger. The playground monitor came over and looked at Josh's finger.

"I think you should let the nurse look at that," she said.

"O.K.," said Josh, and went off to see the nurse, Miss Marcie.

Miss Marcie looked at Josh's finger very carefully. "I think I can fix that," she said.

She took a pair of tweezers and dipped them into something she called antiseptic, and in two minutes, she had the splinter out. Then she washed Josh's hand and put big, white band aid on it.

"Thank you," said Josh. "That feels much better. That was very hard work. Would you say that you have the hardest job of all?"

Miss Marcie peered at Josh over her spectacles.

"I take care of a lot of children every day. They have stomachaches, and toothaches, and sometimes even broken bones. That's hard work it's true, but I wouldn't say it's the hardest job of all," answered Miss Marcie.

"O.K.," said Josh, I'll keep looking."

After lunch Josh had art class. Today was finger painting day, and though they tried to be careful, the class got lots of paint on the floor. When all the pictures were hung up to dry, and Josh and his classmates had hung up their aprons and washed their hands, Mrs. Johnson called the janitor Mr. Simpson, to come and clean up the paint. He came with his big mop and bucket and in five minutes, he had cleaned up all the paint.

"Mr. Simpson," Josh called as he started to leave, "That was very hard work. Would you say your job was the hardest job of all?"

"You kids can really make some big messes." That's true," he said, nodding his head. "I have to clean the boy's bathroom and the girl's bathroom and the lunchroom when all you kids are finished eating. That's pretty hard. But, no, I wouldn't say it was the hardest job of all."

"O.K." said Josh. "I guess I have to keep looking."

Finally three o'clock came and Daddy arrived to pick Josh up at school. Josh smiled. Of course! It was Daddy! Daddy went to work in a big office. He talked on the phone and wrote down numbers, saw people he called clients, and worked on a computer. It had to be Daddy.

Daddy? Josh asked. Do you have the hardest job of all?"

Daddy ruffled Josh's hair. "Well, let me think," he said. It's true I work hard to earn money to take care of you, Tina, Mom, and little Betsy. Sometimes I'm on the phone all day long trying to straighten out problems between companies but Josh, I don't think I have the hardest job of all.

"Oh," Josh said disappointed.

"What's wrong?" asked Daddy.

"Nothing," I was just sure it was you," answered Josh.

"Well," Daddy said with a smile. Just keep looking. I'm sure you'll find the right person soon."

"O.K." said Josh. But he didn't think so.

When they reached home, Mom was standing in the driveway.

"You have to park over there," she said. "Tina has her friends over and the garage is all filled."

She gestured then, just like Mr. Jackson, the policeman.

"Thanks, Honey," said Daddy. Then they all went into the house. Soon as they closed the front door, Tina called Mom over. She and three of her friends sat at the dining room table studying.

"Mom? Can you help us with this? We don't understand this problem," said Tina.

"Sure" Mom said, and she sat down and started explaining the problem.

Gosh, thought Josh, just like my teacher Mrs. Johnson.

Later on at dinner, Mom asked Josh, "did you find the hardest worker today?"

No, said Josh sadly. Everyone I talked to said their job wasn't the hardest."

"Really," even your teacher, Mrs. Johnson?"

"Even Mrs. Johnson," answered Josh sadly.

"Don't give up. You'll find the right person, soon, I'm sure," said Mom.

Just then Betsy started crying.

"She bit her finger, Mom, instead of her carrot. See, her finger's all red," said Tina.

Mom picked up Betsy, and took her to the bathroom, where she washed her finger and doctored it all the while comforting her. Josh looked at the baby's bandaged finger, when Mom brought her back to the table. Just like Miss Marcie, he thought.

Later on everyone was in the family room watching TV except Mom. Josh went to find her. He found her in the kitchen mopping the floor.

"Mom, come watch TV with us," he called.

"I'll be right in, Honey, just as soon as I wipe the table off."

Josh thought to himself, Mom is cleaning up just like Mr. Simpson. Later on that night, they were all playing Monopoly when the phone rang. Mom answered. She was on the phone a long time.

"Who was that, Honey?" asked Dad.

"It was the gardener," answered Mom. "I had to explain just what we needed planted tomorrow and where to plant it."

"Thanks, Honey," said Dad, "for taking care of that."

She straightens things out on the phone, just like Daddy, thought Josh. Suddenly he jumped up.

"Mom!!" he yelled. "It's you!"

"What?" Mom laughed surprised.

"It's you! You have the hardest job of all!"

"But," Mom said. "I just take care of the people I love."

"You direct traffic like Mr. Jackson, you taught Tina like Mrs. Johnson, you fixed Betsy's finger like Miss Marcie, you cleaned the kitchen like Mr. Simpson, the janitor, and you straighten things out over the phone like Daddy. Your the hardest worker.

"You sure are!" said Daddy smiling.

Then they all hugged Mom, and Josh went to bed that night with a big smile on his face.

The End

THE HOUSE

THE HOUSE

IT WAS A humid June morning, when Kate first saw the house.

The sun was high in the sky and the haziness descended previewing another hot day. There was no breeze of which to speak of and already rivulets of moisture were forming on the nape of her neck. There it sat a little house surrounded in shadows. When she stepped into the yard, she could swear she detected a slight breeze blowing. Bordered on all sides by trees and hedges, and lush, emerald green grass perched the house. Near the front door some proud owner had built a platform around an apple tree, and cleared a perfect oval for flower planting.

The house itself was just as small inside, as it appeared outside. Two small bedrooms, a tiny living room and kitchen, all on one floor and even with the bright sun, all the rooms appeared shadowed and dim.

The realtor who was showing Kate the house seemed anxious to be on her way. She pointed out the cellar. The cellar was dark and damp and one tiny locked room proved to be an old cistern. As she relocked the door, a stray cobweb brushed her head causing her to jump nervously. She ushered Kate back into the brighter part of the cellar where a lone bulb dangled from the ceiling. Hastily she pointed out the furnace and then hurried back upstairs and outside. She explained the service contract to Kate and how to operate the garage door while standing in the yard. Then carelessly she handed Kate the keys.

"Look, I know you want to look the house over more carefully than this, so just drop these off at my office when you get back into town and let me know what you think. I have two more appointments this afternoon, but I'll be back by four."

With that, she jumped into her little blue Volkswagen and took off leaving a whiff of Chanel #5.

Kate grasped the keys and slowly gazed at the little house. The sun was now glinting off the upper windows and for just a second, she thought she saw an image shimmering in the glass. When she moved closer for a better look, there was nothing there. That must be the attic Kate thought. She didn't show me that. Well, I'm going to see it now Carefully Kate unlocked the door and went through each room again, slowly now, paring het furniture in place, the bright yellow shed paint the kitchen and the new curtains she'd hang in the living room.

Now, she thought, I'm going to look at the attic. After careful searching, she finally discerned a trap door in the smaller bedroom. She reached up, grasped the chain, and pulled. The door opened and a ladder fell down creaking and groaning. Kate climbed up the dusty steps carefully holding the sides of the ladder. At the top she looked around.

Motes of dust were swirling in the sunlight. The whole area was covered in dirt and so small, she couldn't stand erect. There were several dusty trunks laying around. Other than that, the room was empty. There were four windows, but they were so caked with grime, she couldn't see out. So much for the image she thought she had seen. Kate climbed back down into the small bedroom, pushed up the ladder and pulled the door shut. What a mess she thought, as she brushed off her hands. Still there is something here intriguing to me.

In the yard again, she gazed at the acres of grass with delight. On her way to get a closer look at the garage, she stumbled over what appeared to be a board, jutting out of the ground. Upon closer inspection, she discovered it was the entrance to a root cellar. Stretching out on the soft carpet of grass, Kate smiled. I want this place, she thought. It's just the place for me to write, so quiet and peaceful. I'm sure John will love it too, though he's rarely home long enough to enjoy anywhere these days.

Kate couldn't understand why she felt such an affinity with the place. Even now she felt reluctant to leave, but finally she made sure everything was locked, gathered up her keys, and drove off, still glancing openly at the property in her rearview mirror as it slowly disappeared from sight.

Later on that evening Kate described the house to John in glowing terms, and when she had this total attention, she played her trump card. The price.

"You must be joking," John replied, "Or there must be something wrong with the house."

"No, no" Kate answered. "It's perfect. We'll go tomorrow and you can see for yourself."

"I start a new run tomorrow but I trust your judgment, answered John. "Go for it."

"But don't you want to see for yourself?" Kate asked.

I can see already that your entranced with the place and if you like it that's fine with me," answered John.

Kate felt a knawing disappointment in his disinterest, but she wanted the house, so all she said was "O.K. John, I'll tell Miss Simpson we'll take it."

Two weeks later Kate stood tiredly contemplating the boxes of bric-a-brac and clothes still left to unpack. She was so proud of her home. Every corner sparkled with the work and love Kate had put into it. John had even pitched in and painted the kitchen a bright, cheery, yellow and had cut the acres of grass with not a word of complaint.

Just yesterday he started another cross country run in his truck, so Kate was left to put the rest of the essentials away by herself. As she sat down on the floor in the larger bedroom, she busily folded and stacked her clothes in one pile and John's in the other. She had just emptied the second box when she heard a child's voice coming from the backyard.

Kate stood up and ran to the window. Sure enough, dancing around the apple tree was a beautiful little girl about seven or eight. She wore a faded blue, sleeveless pinafore that barely reached the tops of her knees. Long caramel-colored legs pumped up and down as she pranced back and forth around the tree. Her feet were bare and from where Kate stood, they looked pretty dirty. Her long, dark hair twirled and bounced on her shoulders as she played, and she was humming. It sounded like Ashes, Ashes, We All Fall Down.

Kate hurried to the back door. "Oh, little girl," she called. "Come here."

The little girl looked up and smiled. God, Kate thought she is enchanting. Now that she was standing still, Kate could see that her arms were also very dirty and there were even smudges on her forehead. What mother would let her little girl go out like that, Kate wondered. I'm going to find out where that girl lives and—But the minute Kate opened the door, the little girl looked directly at Kate and smiled again. Then she lifted her hand to wave and vanished. Kate stood staring, her hand still frozen in an answering wave. She ran out the door and around the tree but the little girl was gone. Nervously Kate walked back to the house. I must find out where she lives, thought Kate. She must live around here.

Kate no longer felt like working. She was strangely disturbed by the disappearance of the girl. She took a book, and a glass of iced tea and went to sit on her porch. And though Kate wouldn't admit it, she was hoping to catch another glimpse of the little girl. It was warm and comfortable out there in the old rocker. She tried valiantly to read, but suddenly she felt so tired. The words on the page blurred and faded and soon Kate was fast asleep.

And then she was back in her house. It was her house, but it looked different. The house itself looked newer but the furniture was old and rickety. Two people, a man and a woman were sitting at a scarred, old table in the kitchen and they were arguing.

"You know how broke we are, yet you persist in stopping at that bar," the woman yelled.

"I'm entitled to some enjoyment," the man answered. "I work just as hard as you."

"But look at this place," she retorted. "The furniture is falling apart, and Annette has to wear rags to school."

"I am not giving up my beer," growled the man as he slammed his hand down on the table.

In Kate's dream, she could now see into the small bedroom. A little girl sat huddled on the bed. She had the pillow wrapped around her ears, and she was crying. Every time the voices rose in the kitchen, she burrowed deeper in the bed. Finally, she hopped out of bed, ran to the window, pushed it up a little further and then slipped through to the yard outside.

Kate awoke with a start. What a strange dream, she thought. She was aware of a terrible feeling of sadness, but she didn't know why.

The next day, Kate drove to town to replenish her supply of groceries. On the way home, she stopped at several houses that bordered hers to inquire about the young girl. No one knew of any children until she reached the last house, several miles away from her own. Ella and Tim Roberts, a nice elderly couple lived there comfortably retired. Ella gasped as Kate described the girl.

"A small, darked haired girl, you say, you couldn't have seen her. You just couldn't have. Not that little girl."

"Why not?" asked Kate. "She was playing in the yard and having a wonderful time."

"There was a family that lived in your house once", whispered the old lady. "It was about forty years ago. The father and mother bickered a lot, but the little girl was like a ray of sunshine. Always laughing and dancing about, and kind to every living thing. She looked just like the girl you described."

"This couldn't be her", Kate said. "That said would be a woman now."

Oh no, Ella replied, That little girl wouldn't. The whole family died tragically.

"What happened?" asked Kate.

Well, they say her folks was having one of them arguments I was telling you about. The little girl use to get upset when they did that and she ran and hid somewhere. Well, when they were leaving to go to work the next day, they couldn't find her so's they just left without her. About a mile from town they hit a ten-wheeler and were killed instantly."

"Oh no", whispered Kate.

"Yep," said Ella. "Then when someone finally thought about the little girl, they couldn't find her. Weeks later a farmer found his dog nosing around the yard. He couldn't get him to leave. It was then they found the little girl dead on the root cellar. She had climbed in there to hide like she often did, but this time the latch had slipped and she couldn't get out and no one thought of looking there until it was too late."

"But that's horrible", cried Kate.

"It shore is", said Ella. "And that aint all. They say that little girl still plays around that old house. Some folks have seen her. They say your house is haunted."

"Well, that's a sad story", answered Kate. "But this is not that little girl. I'd swear she was flesh and blood. She smiled at me and I saw her as clear

as I see you."

"Well", Ella said. "Your gonna believe what you believe. But I'd be very careful, that's all."

Two nights later, when John returned, he and Kate were sitting on the porch sipping cold frosted glasses of lemonade. Somewhere in the darkness, an owl was hooting mournfully. The smell of lilacs scented the warm night air. Kate sighed and then very softly she whispered, "John I want to have a baby."

"Now, Kate, I don't think we're ready for that yet."

"Kate sat up abruptly, "Not ready. What do you mean? First, we had to wait until we were financially stable. Then we have to wait until had more room. Well, we have acres of room now. How can we not be ready?

John shifted uncomfortably. "I want to be home with you when we have a child. Not traveling around the highways worried about you. Bes your so isolated out here. I'd worry about you all the time."

"And when would that be? Kate asked, "When would you be home with me John?"

"Soon as I get a nest egg. Then I could get a job in town. I'd be home with you every night. I'd be with you through the whole pregnancy."

"John, you know that will never happen. You'll never have enough to satisfy you. And I'll never have a child.

"Now Kate, you get upset too easy". John stood and pulled Kate closer. "I promise it won't be much longer.

Kate stared out into the dark yard. Tears shimmered in her eyes. But all she said was "All right John, we'll wait a little longer." Out there in the darkness, she saw a flash of light. But when she looked closer it disappeared. Must be heat lightning, she thought, as she and John went in. After that night, there was a wall between the two of them. Kate went about her daily chores and John went about his, but a lot of the closeness between the two of them was lost.

One month crept slowly by with this coldness between the two of them. Then one afternoon as Kate washed clothes in the basement, a storm blew up. Kate reached the kitchen with her freshly dried clothes just as a tremendous clap of thunder shook the windows.

"Oh no", she whispered, running to the door. Dark clouds scudded across the sky. In the distance she saw flashes of lightning. Kate was petrified of thunderstorms. When any sign of a storm appeared, Kate would go to any area where there were people around so she could hide her fear in the noise and confusion of others. Now she had waited too long and she was trapped alone in the house with a hideous storm clamoring about. She tentatively took a step out the door. Thunder crashed again, and rain exploded out of the sky. Too late, she thought, as she raced to the smaller bedroom, where there was only one small window. Flinging herself on the single bed, she covered her head with the pillow, shaking every time the lightning flashed or thunder rumbled. Moaning and shaking, Kate slowly became aware of a soft stroking of her hair.

"Don't be afraid, Kate", a soft voice murmured next to her ear. Kate glanced up fearfully and there sat the little girl she had seen in the yard. Lightning flashed again in the darkened room, as the little girl moved closer and sat down next to Kate.

"Who are you?" whispered Kate.

"My name is Annette, but everyone calls me Annie," answered the little girl. "I heard you crying, and I came to stay with you until the storm is over."

"But where did you come from?" asked Kate.

"I don't know. I guess I've always been here", said Annie.

"Where are your parents?" persisted Kate.

I don't know. I can't find them anymore", said Annie sadly. "But you look a lot like my mom. Do you think you could be my mom?" she asked.

Kate put her arms around Annie and hugged her tightly. Then Annie ran to the closet and pulled from a shelf a checker game.

"We can play this until the storm is over", she said smiling.

Kate and Annie played for hours in the small bedroom. Every once in a while, Kate would caress the soft, brown curls so close to her. Sometime after eight, Kate realized how quiet it was. The storm had passed, and she hadn't even noticed. Kate yawned.

Annie said, "You lay down. I'll stay until you fall asleep."

Kate smiled, "I just want to rest my eyes a minute. Then we'll play some more."

When Kate opened her eyes again bright sunlight was streaming in the window and Annette was gone. But Kate felt such a feeling of contentment and she knew Annette would come back whenever she wished for her. What a delightful girl she thought. They had talked for hours, and played ten games of checkers. Kate wasn't a fool. She realized Annette must be a ghost. But if so, she was the sweetest ghost Kate had ever seen, and she would tell no one because she wanted Annette to visit again.

During the weeks that followed, Kate and Annie grew closer. They explored the woods together behind the house, and they played jump rope under the apple tree. Kate would even pack picnic lunches to eat in the yard, though Annie never really ate, it was fun to pretend. Often, they would play games in what used to be Annie's room. Feeling foolish, she had made Annie several dresses, which she took great pains to hide from John. On the days when John was home, Annette would not appear, and on those days, Kate sometimes doubted her sanity. Was she really playing whole days with a little girl that wasn't real? Kate wondered.

John had noticed a difference in Kate also. After the baby discussion, she seemed depressed and withdrawn. Then one day he'd come home, and she was humming a nursery rhyme and baking. At first, he was pleased at the change in her spirit, until he'd caught her whispering near the root cellar. When he confronted her, she said she thought she heard some animal in there. But John had watched her for a long time before he'd called. She'd been having a conversation with someone he couldn't see. Also, in t e past, whenever he'd left on one of his trips, she'd been sad when he left. Now he could sense her eagerness for him to be on his way. But why? Who was she talking to? John began to worry.

So worried, that the very next day, he paid a visit to the town library. As he approached the desk, one of the librarians came forward.

"What can I do for you, sir?" she asked brightly.

John shifted awkwardly from foot to foot. "I just want to check through some of your old newspapers."

"Why certainly sir", she answered. "Our reference section is back near the window. Is there any particular year you're interested in?'

Nervously John cleared his throat. "I ah—no, I just wanted to check through some earlier dated papers."

"Well, this group", she said, pointing out the microfiche machine go from 1900 to present time. Let me know if you need any help sir." Then she walked back to the main desk, her heels clicking loudly on the mezzanine. John sat down at the microfiche machine and soon he was flipping through newspapers like a pro. He had no idea what he was looking for, but during his few trips to town, he'd heard some rumors about the house he lived in. He had classified them as foolish, until he recently noticed Kate in the yard, having private conversations with no one he could see. Still feeling decidedly uncomfortable, John was about to leave when a paper flipped by showing a picture of his house. Above the picture huge, glaring headlines read TWO KILLED

IN CRASH – DAUGHTER FOUND DEAD. The paper was dated June 5th, 1959.

"My God", John whispered. "A little girl found dead and in that root cellar. Her whole family dead. How horrible."

John sat stunned. Unconsciously he flipped the remaining papers over when his hand froze again. There on the screen his house was pictured again and this time the headline read WOMAN FOUND NEAR DEATH IN ROOT CELLAR. The woman claimed she'd talked to a little girl. She had no idea she'd been down there two whole days, and even on the way to the hospital she was still asserting that she was fine.

John felt the blood drain from his face. His hands trembled violently as he turned off the viewer. Thoroughly rattled, he stumbled clumsily out of the library and back to his car. He sat there for a half hour feeling numb. Then slowly he drove home.

"Now what?" he thought as he drove. Confront Kate and tell her the house idolizes so much is haunted?

As he drove up, he spotted Kate immediately. She was busily pulling weeds from the flower bed. She had on ragged shorts and a faded, blue sleeveless shirt which clung to her petite five-foot-tall body. She had tied her long reddish-brown curls back in a ponytail which only enhanced her youthful appearance. John hoisted his six-foot frame slowly out of the car dreading the task ahead. Kate leaped up and flew into his arms dirt and all.

"Honey, your back early," she said. "Is everything all right?"

John guided her to their favorite spot on the porch. "Sit down Kate," he said. "I've something to tell you."

Kate sat. John looked so worried. Her gentle John. People were always surprised how someone so huge could be so docile.

"I've just left the library; Kate and I've discovered a lot of bad things about this house. A little girl died here, and her mother and father were killed not far from here."

Kate smiled and said. "I know all that, John."

John stared at her. "You know, but you never said—

"I knew even before we bought the house John," she answered.

"Then why did you want to move here?" asked John

"Simply because I loved the house. I still do. Don't you, John?"

"Kate, it's not safe. It can't be. I also read about a woman who was found trapped in that root cellar. Did you know about that?" asked John.

"No, answered Kate. "I didn't know that. But I heard the rumors about the house being haunted, when I went into town. I'm happy here, John and I thought you were too."

"Yes Kate, I've been happy here but now that you know the truth. Aren't you afraid? Don't you want to move?" asked John.

Kate said nothing for a few minutes. Then she grasped John and turned him around. "Look, John," she whispered. Do you think I want to leave this?"

John looked. A carpet of sweet-smelling grass covered the yard. Two robins had built a home over the garage and were chirping nosily. The lilac bushes were in bloom and their sweet perfume floated in the air. All the flowers blossomed and now a rainbow of color surrounded the house. John understood. His Katie poured her love into this place. Now she was part of it and it was part of her. She'd made the house a home.

"O.K. Kate, I understand. That's not going to keep me from worrying about you. I can see you don't want to move. What are we going to do? asked John.

"I don't know but I don't want to move, John," Kate whispered.

After much discussion, John consented to remain in the house providing Kate agree to two stipulations. The first one was to have the root cellar cemented over as soon as possible. The second was that Kate call him at the first sign of anything unusual. Meanwhile, he redoubled his efforts to secure a job in town. He made sure that he took only runs that were in the surrounding territory and he started checking all areas of the house and the yard each night before going to bed.

Several nights later, Kate awoke to a strange light flickering in the yard. She glanced at John who was extra vigilant lately, but he was still sleeping soundly. Quietly she pulled her slippers on and grabbed her bathrobe. Maybe it was Annie. She stepped cautiously into the yard. Down at the end of the drive, John parked the truck to save time in the morning, so he could spend more time with Kate. Kate noticed the strange light seemed to originate directly behind the huge truck. Kate circled carefully around the truck and suddenly she saw them, a man and a woman standing in a circle of light just ahead. Kate's heart clamored in alarm, and even as her mouth opened of its own volition to scream, somewhere in the horror crawling through her mind, she realized these two were uncannily familiar. Her shriek echoed across the quiet night, but no sign of movement came from the house, so Kate had no recourse but to turn and face these supernatural beings.

The woman spoke first Kate, don't fear us. Look at us. You know who we are. It was I that sent you the dream one afternoon, so you would know why our Annie remains here so lost and confused in this realm.

Then the man spoke, "Yes, we bickered and wasted our time on earth never knowing it would be over so quickly. Now we remain separated in death. Our daughter lingers here earthbound seeking love from anyone who occupies this space because she never received it from us in life."

Kate, whose trembling knees no longer held her, sank down on the grass. "Why have you come back?" she asked.

The woman smiled. "You know why, Kate. Why do you tremble before us and yet you play with Annie day after day and she is just as much a specter as we are. You wish and dream for a child and our sweet Annie fills all the requirements."

The man walked around the truck and looked sadly at Kate.

"This truck is just like the one that killed us", he said. We are allowed back one night, to relive our useless death and to plead with you to send our Annie to us."

"Yes," the woman replied. "Out of all the people who have lived here, Annie loves you the best. She'll listen to you."

Kate sat crying openly, "I can't send her away. I love her." When Kate looked up the woman seemed to be fading.

"Kate", she whispered. "We have no more time. Please send our daughter to us."

The man's voice echoed eerily as they disappeared, "Please Kate."

Kate stood up shakily, "I don't know how to send her away" she whispered but the spectral couple had vanished, When she reached the bedroom, John slept on soundly. She crawled back into bed and lay there sniffling quietly the rest of the night. The next morning, John was forced to take a run that kept him away overnight. He gave Kate scads of instructions on how to contact him and still he was reluctant to leave. Finally, he left and Kate was free to indulge in her misery.

Kate was sniffling into the pillow still, when she felt a feather-like touch on her head. Thank God, she thought my Annie.

"What's wrong Kate?" Annie asked. "Why are you crying?"

"I just missed you, Annie", admitted Kate. "I missed you, that's all."

"Well let's pick some strawberries and have a picnic. You know I can't come when John's here", whispered Annie.

"I know", answered Kate. "Come on, let's go."

All day they played. They roamed the woods together. Took a swim in the brook. Had their picnic on the hillside, and then late afternoon Kate knew she had to tell the little girl the truth. They were sitting on their favorite spot, the porch and Annie was trying to weave daisies into her

curls.

"Annie", Kate said. "I have to tell you something. You know, Annie that being here with me is not where you're supposed to be.

"Sure it is, Kate", replied Annie. "We have fun.

"No Annie, try to remember. Where were you when you couldn't find your parents anymore?"

"My parents?" "You're my mom, Kate, retorted Annie,

"NO, Annie, I'm not. You know that. Where were you?"

"Well", Annie wrinkled her nose. "I think I hid in the root cellar and when I came out everyone was gone.

"Do you think they just left you? asked Kate.

"I don't think so. First, I was in the cellar, and I couldn't get out and then I was very hungry and cold and then I thought I saw a bright light but I could see my house too, and I didn't want to leave. I wanted to live here with my mommy and daddy and be happy. After I waited awhile, they did come but when I tried to make the lady stay with me, they went away.'

"Annie", whispered Kate. The only way you can go to your real mommy and daddy is if you go to that light.

"Kate, no, I can't find the light anymore," mumbled Annie. Can't you stay with me? All you have to do is stay with me in the root cellar light goes away. Then we can be together forever."

Kate hugged the little girl. So young to never know genuine love in her short life. She deserved her true parents.

"Look, Honey", Kate said. "I won't do that. I love John and I must stay with him, but I'll help you find your parents. We will have to go back in that cellar just for a little while. Then I'm sure they will come for you."

Annie clung to Kate for a long time. She roamed this yard for years searching for her parents. Maybe it was time to go. "All right, Kate", she said, "Let's go, I'm ready."

Kate shuddered as she unlatched the cellar door and started down those dark steps. She took a flashlight and peered around the small enclosed area. Cobwebs hung down in long, filmy strands. Dust floated in the sunlight. Annie settled on the bottom step, and Kate sat down too. Small spiders crawled along the wall, and the place smelled like fermented grapes. Tomorrow the men were coming to cement this place over, so if this didn't work, Kate had no idea what to do.

"I think Kate, that we have to close the door. That's how it was that night", ventured Annie.

"You know Annie, I think you're right", said Kate as she reached up and pulled the trap door shut. Then fearfully, she reached back up again to make it sure it was unlocked. When she felt it lift, she gave a sigh of relief. Then she and Annie talked and waited.

Hours later, Kate woke abruptly. How could she fall asleep? It was pitch black in the cellar and she fumbled nervously for the flashlight. With the light she saw Annie still sitting, but she seemed unaware of Kate. She started at a spot on the wall and when Kate followed her gaze, she saw it too. A small spot of light which kept enlarging and getting brighter and suddenly the whole cellar gleamed with a brilliant bright light.

"Come Annie, we're waiting for you." called a voice.

Now Annie could see a face materializing in the center of the light. Her mother.

"Mommy", she yelled. She stood up and scrambled to the radiant light.

"Come Annie", her father called.

"I'm coming", she yelled.

Then she moved away into the brightness, almost transparent as the luminous light enveloped her. At the last moment, she turned back and whispered, "Goodbye Kate, I love you", and then she was gone.

Kate sat stunned for a few minutes. Then on cramped aching legs she struggled to the top, and pushed on the door. It did not move. No, no, thought Kate, I checked it. It was unlocked. Still, it did not budge. Kate struggled frantically for hours and then collapsed into tears. She was so tired. She hadn't slept at all last night and now she was exhausted. I'll just rest my eyes for a minute, was her last conscious thought.

John edged the speedometer up to seventy, and prayed there were no troopers lurking about. He was on his way home and he was anxious about Kate. He'd called her twice and listened to his own voice telling him no one was home. The roadside sign ahead read twenty miles to Allentown. Not much farther. Thank God. As John turned on the highway for home, sheets of rain erupted from the ominous gray clouds overhead.

In her prison, Kate shivered as cold, wet rain slid between the slats above and dripped slimy mud splatters on her neck and arms. The slits of light which sifted through the cracks were now darkening and dusk was falling again. She'd been down here all night and all day. Frantically, Kate banged on the roof again and again and then dissolved into fear on the floor of her cell. She sobbed so loudly, she almost missed the growl of the truck engine as John swerved carelessly into the driveway.

"Kate", he was yelling. "Kate, where are you?"

The kitchen door slammed and in seconds, she heard him calling in the yard. Kate opened her mouth to scream but nothing came out but a hoarse croak. It didn't matter. John was already there.

"Kate, I know your there", he yelled. "Get back to the side. I have to chop this open." THACK, THACK, THACK, he chopped at the door and then glorious light flooded her cave. Then John picked her up and hugged her close.

"I knew you were in trouble. We're leaving this place once and for all. I almost lost you today, John mumbled as he carried her to the house. When they reached the kitchen, Kate grabbed his arm tightly and squeezed.

"John, look", she yelled. "Look!!!

Even in the approaching dusk and gray, rainy afternoon, some new light emanated from the yard or was it the house. No matter. The shadows were gone as if all sadness was erased from the house.

"We don't have to move, Honey", Kate whispered. "Can't you feel it? The darkness is gone."

John smiled gently at his Kate. He'd agree with anything she said as long as she was safe. He carried her to the bath, started the water for her, and when she seemed to be fine, prepared a quick supper for them. They ate in the bedroom, Kate wrapped up in her old fuzzy robe. When they'd finished eating, John said. "Well, I better clean up this mess."

"Honey", Kate whispered. "Forget the dishes. Stay with me." John climbed into bed with Kate and immediately, she kissed him.

"Kate, sweetheart, don't you think you ought to rest", John murmured.

"This is the best medicine I could have", said Kate teasingly. John needed no further invitation. Much later Kate smiled at her snoring husband. At last the closeness between them was back. In fact, the atmosphere of the whole house had changed. The ghosts were put to rest. Kate drifted back to sleep lulled by the rhythmic pattering of the rain. The next day the men came and concreted over the root cellar. Although Kate knew there was no need to, John insisted.

Several weeks passed and during this time, John was hired at a job in town as a forklifter. Kate continued to work away in her garden and had finally started writing. Still from time to time she missed Annie.

One day in late June, John arrived home before Kate. As John prepared a surprise supper for Kate and himself, he realized with a jolt they'd been living here for a year. We can make this a celebration he thought.

Kate drove home in record time. Jumping out of the car, she headed for the house at a run.

"John'", she yelled as she flew through the back door. "John, I've something to tell you." John grabbed her as she sailed past the table.

"What is it Honey? John asked. trample your Petunias?" "What could possibly make you trample your Petunias?"

"I'm pregnant", she shouted. "I had an appointment today in town, and the doctor confirmed it. I am pregnant!!"

"That's wonderful, sweetheart, replied John. "That's perfect. A little boy or girl to make our lives complete. You've made me so happy, Kate. We sure have a lot to celebrate tonight."

"It's going to be a girl", Kate said with a smile.

John laughed and said, "Kate, you couldn't possible know already."

"It's going to be a girl," insisted Kate. 'A sweet little girl with huge dark eyes and long curly brown hair. I KNOW and I'm going to call her ANNETTE!!!"

THE MAGIC GARDEN

ONCE UPON A time in a kingdom far away lived an old witch named Coraline in an old castle surrounded by tall pine trees. For many years she lived in the castle feared and hated by the people of the countryside. She hated the peasants that lived near her castle, so she plotted and schemed up a plan to make them even more miserable. She decided to plant a huge garden, an enchanted garden. But even enchanted gardens take lots of work to make them grow, so she would force the peasants from the countryside to work in it. The first two peasants to get caught in her web were Dono and Dano. They had sneaked past the castle to fish in the forest and when they trotted back happily swinging the three trout they had caught, the witch spotted them. Dono and Dano were the cowards of the village so when the witch yelled you halt there, they trembled and cried. Then they tried to give the witch their fish so she would let them go. But the witch said "I caught you fair and square and now you must stay and toil in my garden." Dono and Dano pleaded and wept but the witch pushed them into the garden and slammed the iron gate. She threw in garden tools and seeds and all the things needed to plant a garden. "Now get to work", she yelled and she locked the huge gate and returned to the castle.

The next villager to be caught by the witch was Princess Stepho. She was so conceited, she would stop along the paths trying to see her reflection in the leaves or rain puddles and she spent all day combing her long blonde tresses. She was squeezing berry juice on her lips and trying to see her reflection in the lake, when the witch suddenly appeared behind her.

"You'll be a welcome addition to my garden", she cackled. "You can arrange the shells around my vegetables." Then she threw her black cloak over Princess Stepho's head and they both disappeared.

Now the other villagers were worried. All their countrymen were vanishing. They made a vow to stay away from the witch's territory. They stuck with their vow too until Picnic Day. On Picnic Day all the people would gather in the village square. They would hold games and dancing, display their crafts and eat. Whole chickens and pigs roasted in the glen and all sorts of vegetables and desserts would cover the platform built around the square. Chero, who was always mischievous by nature convinced old sweet Bono to go with her into the forest to find wild chestnuts and pick berries for the pies. The witch who'd been waiting for more silly villagers to cross her path, swooped down in her big, black cape and spirited them away in seconds. After Bono and Chero disappeared, the rest of the village were so upset they canceled the Picnic Day.

Kimo and Leno, two of the bravest villagers, decided to rescue their friends and get rid of the witch once and for all. That very night, they slipped through the gate crawling in the shadows until they heard the witch retire to the tower room and all was quiet. Then they searched the castle for their friends. Through long, dark hallways they tiptoed. Even though Kimo and Leno were the bravest of the village, they trembled every time a stray rat rustled by or a bat fluttered overhead. Finally, they came upon a room where an eerie green light shone. On the door, huge letters spelled out POTION ROOM.

"Let's check in here", Kimo whispered.

In the room were rows of shelves and bottles of all sizes and shapes on everyone. Along the floor boxes of all kinds of usual plants sat. What really scared Leno though, were the two bottles full of strange liquid sitting on the table right in front of them.

"Look", Leno whispered. "She has the garden sprayer all set up. And these two bottles of stuff. She's going to spray it in the garden."

"What is it?" asked Kimo. "Can you read the bottles?"

Leno climbed up on the huge table for a closer look. "This one says Heart's Desire and that one over there says End of Dreams."

"That;s it", whispered Kimo excitedly. "She's going to use that End of dreams stuff and feed it to us. Then none of us will have lives anymore. We'll just be her servants."

"What can we do?" asked Leno.

"I know", answered Kimo. "We can switch the bottles. "The other will give us our Heart's Desire. The witch will never know until it's too late. Hurry, let's do it before daylight."

So Kimo and Leno switched the bottles, and then they scuttled out of the castle and back to the village before the witch woke up.

The next morning, the witch released the workers from the dungeon. "I have something special for you today. All my fruits and vegetables are blooming. Now is the time to spray them with my magic potion. Now get to work. I want everything sprayed before dusk or I'll turn you all into toads."

By the end of the day, the whole garden was sprayed and Dano was weeping as usual on his side of the dungeon. Princess Steph was trying vainly to get the mud out of fingernails when Kimo suddenly appeared beside her.

"How did you get in here?" she gasped. "Are you going to get us out?"

"I can't. The witch is out there but I have a plan. Last night Leno and I switched the potions. I know she's going to feed it to you but we must somehow get her to eat some of it too."

"What's in the potion?" asked Princess Steph. "Will it make me prettier?"

"I'm not sure what it will do. It was the only thing I could think of to free us from the witch. One of you must come with me to the kitchen so we can put some of the vegetables in her food too."

"I'll come", whispered Dano.

Kimo and Dano sneaked to the kitchen and sure enough, there sat a huge basket of the vegetables on the table. Kimo snatched three tomatoes and several cabbage leaves and stuffed them in the pot of batwings cooking on the old iron stove. Then he grabbed the huge ladle and mixed it in, minutes before the witch crept in. Dano and

Kimo hid behind the wood pile and watched as the old crone cut up vegetables and boiled them in a gigantic vat. When the vegetables were cooked, she ladled them into a large tray and carried it to the dungeon to feed to the peasants. Dano scuttled through the tunnels getting back just ahead of the witch.

"All right peasants, you may now eat some of the vegetables you've worked so hard to grow. You are all going to eat well tonight." said the witch.

"Why are you being nice to us?" asked Chero worriedly.

"Look", yelled the witch. "Eat now, or I'll turn you all into bats."

One by one the villagers ate from the huge tray and then crawled to a spot on the floor where they immediately fell asleep.

"That takes care of them", muttered the witch as she returned to her tower. Later on the night, she had three helpings of her batwing soup never knowing she was eating her own potion. The next morning when the sun rose, beautiful music came from the castle. Chero and Bono were singing. Their voices rang out true and clear. Princess Stepho was twirling around on her toes light as a feather in time to the song. Dono and Dano who had always wanted to be soldiers, stood up brave and valiantly were trying to unlock the gate. Then they all heard a sound on the steps. A lovely, young woman appeared. Dono stepped forward and grasped her hand.

"Who are you fair young princess?" he asked. "Your beauty takes my breath away."

"Oh my handsome soldier. I was the witch. It has always been my dream to be loved by a good-looking young soldier and to be a beautiful princess."

Stepho, who was still twirling on her toes whispered "It must be a spell."

"Yes, said the princess, "but a wonderful spell. Look."

As they looked up the whole castle turned from a dark, dreary place to a lovely place of light and flowers. As if by magic birds began to sing in the trees outside. The wicked witch was gone and everything was good in the village again. Later that day, Dono brought all the villagers to the castle and they tasted the magic vegetables. The next day Dono and the young princess, who they called Coral were married. Together he and the princess ruled over the little village and everyone had their Heart's Desire forever and ever.

64

THE MAGIC RING

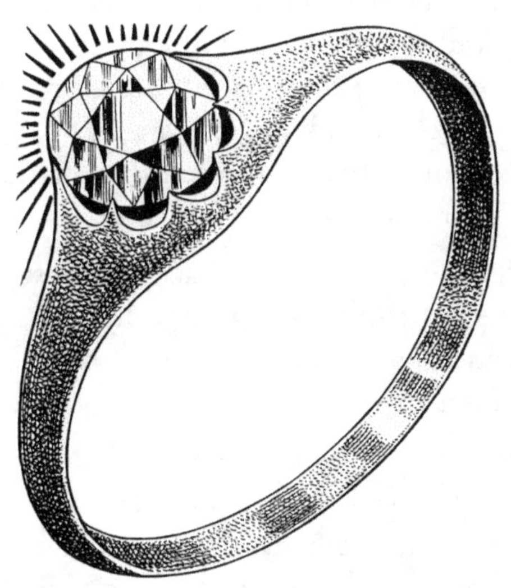

JANE MARIE ANDREWS woke up Monday morning at 6:30 AM feeling very disgusted with herself. Her family had just moved into town and this was to be her first day at a new school. Dragging her 170 lb. 5'3" frame out of bed, she grumbled her way to the bathroom. She peered at her stringy, straight, hair in the mirror and then finished brushing her teeth without looking back again. She grumbled her way through breakfast, though her mom tried to cheer her up and finally, but reluctantly left for school.

She could feel the stares on her back as she stood in line in the office waiting for her schedule and signing admission papers. She could hear the whispers and giggling as she entered her first class and wedged her bulk behind a desk.

Several weeks passed with Jane becoming more miserable everyday. She knew how unattractive she was, but after repeated tries with crash diets which always failed, and fiasco home permanents, Jane had given up. One day in class the teacher asked her to remain after class with Tom Simmons, the all star football player.

"Jane", she said, "I asked you to stay after class because I want to know if you would agree to tutor Tom. He's falling behind in class and since your an A student, well he could certainly use your help."

Tom smiled at her, "Would you Jane?" he asked, "I sure would appreciate your help. If I fall any further behind in English, they may kick me off the football team."

Jane had been ready to say no, but something in his expression made her change her mind. There was no pity in his eyes or amusement He seemed genuinely sincere.

So she forced a smile and said, "Tom, whenever it's convenient for you. I'll tutor you."

Tom, at first, was only being friendly to Jane because he himself sincerely needed her help and though not very attractive, she seemed like a nice enough person. But after a few weeks of working with her he found himself really liking her. She had ways of making him understand that none of his teachers had, and she was really interesting and fun to talk to. He found out that not only was she very intelligent, but she was creative and could talk for hours on just about any topic you one could name. However, she had an inferiority complex a mile wide. He began to wonder how he could get her to make herself feel more attractive, so that she would feel more confident that she was interesting on the outside as she was on the inside.

The solution came in the form of this little pawnshop, he passed on his way to school each morning. One day he saw in the shop window, a very extraordinary ring. It had a large blue oval shaped stone in the center flanked on each side by four seed pearls, and if one looked deep into the stone, it reflected back your images as it changed from one color to another. It was beautiful. Just the thing for Jane's birthday which was coming up soon. The old shopkeeper told Tom it was an old piece of Egyptian Jewelry, all that was left, of what once had been a fabulous set. Then Tom had his brainstorm. He bought the ring for Jane and then took it to an engraver and on the inside band in tiny letters, he had engraved ALL WHO WEAR THIS RING SHALL BECOME BEAUTIFUL.

Two weeks later on her birthday he presented his gift to Jane wrapped in golden paper and tied with a silver bow. Tom watched anxiously as she opened it. Maybe she would be insulted by the message on the ring. When Jane finally lifted the ring from the box, her fingers trembled slightly and then she read the message on the band. Tears glimmered in her eyes.

"Jane?", Tom asked quietly, "Don't you like it? It's an old Egyptian ring and the shopkeeper told me it's enchanted."

"Oh Tom", she whispered, "It's the most beautiful ring I ever saw and I shall never take it off. Do you suppose it really could make me beautiful?"

"To me you are beautiful", Tom said, and then he bent forward and kissed her lightly on the lips.

"Jane", called her mother. "Come and see your cake, and we some presents here for you to open."

"Coming Mother", she answered, as she reluctantly moved out of Tom's arms.

Long after her party ended, and everyone had gone to bed, Jane lay in the darkness looking at this twinkling ring on her finger and finally admitting to herself how much she liked Tom.

"Oh Ring", she whispered to the darkness, "Please do your stuff."

The next morning was Saturday and Jane had made a big decision. She was going to take her birthday money and go to one of the best beauty salons in town and have her hair permed. she had always been afraid to have it done before but now she knew without a doubt, it would be the best thing to do. Too excited to eat, she gulped down a cup of coffee and she was on her way.

She reached Barbara's Beauty Salon in record time, but when she tried to explain to the attendant what she wanted, the lady just smiled.

"Look honey," she said, "there is nothing wrong with your hair. You've just never had a good cut. You have beautiful hair. Just wait until I finish with you."

Two hours later, Jane walked out of the salon another person. Hair which had hung limp and long past her neck before, now tapered just off her neck in soft, glowing, curls all around her head. The hairdresser used a rinse on her hair and it shimmered with blonde highlights. All the way home Jane kept stopping and glancing into store windows to make sure it was her. Even her mother was astounded at the difference.

"Thank you ring'", Jane whispered, just as she slipped off to sleep that night.

Several weeks passed with Jane joining more and more clubs at school and getting to know and actually like more and more people.

Her new hair style gave her confidence and she was actually losing weight. She no longer sat around moping and eating at night and even started going out regularly with Tom. Tom could not get over the change in Jane and found himself falling a little more in love with her every day.

February was just beginning and the whole school was talking about the dance coming up. It was given on Valentines Day and naturally called the sweetheart dance. Jane, even in spite of her new found popularity, did not expect to go, so she was completely flabbergasted when Tom asked her.

"Tom", she said, "I know your trying to be nice but you don't have to take elephant Jane to the dance. I'll understand."

"Jane", Tom answered, "Have you really, really, looked at yourself lately. You've lost weight and you look great. Why you couldn't even be a very anemic elephant. Please say you'll go. I need you there."

"I believe you really mean that Tom", Jane answered, "And if you really want me to go I'd be honored to accompany you", and then she smiled. That night Jane studied herself in the mirror for a long time. She really had lost weight. No wonder her clothes were so loose lately and her hair fell and moved in soft ringlets every time she moved her head. She really had become beautiful and it was all due to the ring that glittered on her finger.

"Oh thank you magic ring," she whispered.

Throwing herself into preparations for the big dance she even joined an exercise class to put the finishing touches on her much improved figure and took to eating lots of salad suppers. But now it wasn't a chore, it was all for Tom, and well worth it when she saw his expression the night of the dance. Jane spent hours choosing just the right dress. It was beautiful, bright red for Valentine's Day, with thin, tiny, spaghetti, straps, gathered tightly at the waist, and flowing out into a wide billowing skirt which came to just below her knees. Her hair was a soft shining cap around her head, and on her feet dainty, red, high, heeled sandals. She had taken careful pains to put on her makeup just right and felt well rewarded when Tom kissed on the cheek and then clasped her hand gently as he led her out the door.

"Jane, you look like a princess tonight and I love you", he said as he placed a corsage of roses on her wrist.

"Oh Tom", she whispered, "Thank you. This has all happened because of the ring you know. And I will always love you for bringing happiness into my life."

Tom glanced at her glowing face and then the ring twinkling on her finger and frowned slightly to himself. The dance was a grand success. Jane was whirled from partner to partner but always reclaimed by Tom, who was loving her more and more by the minute. They danced the last dance together and Jane clung tightly to Tom knowing just how much she had come to love him. On the way home they parked by a small stream. Torn lead her up to the little bridge that spanned the stream and then took her in his arms.

"Jane, I think you know how I feel about you", he whispered in her hair. I know it may be too soon to think about think about this but I hope at you will. Next year after you graduate, I would be honored if you would consent to be my wife."

"Oh Tom", she whispered and reached out to stoke her hand through his hair, but as her hand slid through his hair, her now loosely fitting ring' slipped from her finger and bounced once on the bridge and then fell into the swirling depths of the stream.

Jane became hysterical. She ran off the bridge, slipped and slid down the side of the bank, and knelt in the stream frantically searching for the ring. When she finally stood up, her beautiful, red, dress was soaked to the waist and her dainty red heels were covered in mud. Tom grabbed her all held her tight as tears streamed out of her eyes.

"Oh no", she cried. "Without that ring, I am nothing, nothing. I'll be ugly again, unpopular. Everyone will hate me. Oh, God," she whispered.

"Jane, Jane, listen to me", Tom shouted. "The ring is nothing. The ring means nothing. It was you that changed, YOU. I had those words engraved on the ring. There was never any spell. It was just an old ring, pretty maybe, but that's all. I will buy you another."

Jane stared at him. "You had those words engraved on the ring," she whispered. It was all a story you made up. The ring really wasn't magic."

"Yes", Tom groaned, "I had to get you to care. You were such fun to talk to, but you seemed to hate yourself. I liked you so much. I wanted you to like you too. If you hate me now I understand. The ring was really an old Egyptian piece but the rest I made up."

Jane stared down into the dark churning, water for a long time and then she stepped closer to Tom and wrapped both arms around his waist.

"I would love to be your wife," she said with a smile, whenever you want and thank you Tom, for showing me the true meaning of love. I don't think I'll ever feel ugly again. I do love you so much but if I'm ever afraid". . . .

"If you are ever afraid", Tom said, closing his arms around her, "I'll be there to help you, guide you, and love you for the rest of your life." Then Tom pulled her close and kissed her sealing between them the secret of The Magic Ring.

THE MAN IN THE MIST

THE MOURNFUL SOUND of the wind howled. Fog drifted down upon the town like a large gray blanket. The night was silent except for the eerie sound of the wind. It seemed as if all the woodland creatures had suddenly disappeared. Not even an owl broke the silence. The fog moved and pulsed like a living thing. It thickened and twisted forming ominous shapes. The wind reached a high keening wail as if it were crying. A sound started like a roaring freight train coming closer and closer. When the sound reached the level of thunder, he stepped out of the fog.

He was clothed all in black. His huge hat slanted over his face revealing only his eyes. His clothing was all dark and around his shoulders, he wore a long, dark cape. He moved along in a gliding motion not making a sound. Skimming along in swinging gait, he moved forward, his feet barely touching the ground. He paused at the end of the forest when he reached the clearing. The fog cloud which had surrounded him and shadowed his movements, suddenly floated away like a wisp of smoke. In the distance he spotted his destination, a tiny cottage nestled among the trees at the very end of the road.

Standing by the cottage window, Lori suddenly experienced a great feeling of wonder and a tiny stirring of fear, and she knew he had returned—

Lori Brown was a dreamer. Everyone in the village knew it. She was sixteen years old, quiet, unassuming and she loved to read. Her shoulder length auburn hair rimmed a round face which even years later, kept her looking perpetually young. She was a very likable girl, and usually alert until her hazel eyes filmed over, she'd stare into space and become the heroine in one of her day dreams. For the most part though, she did well in her studies and lived a relatively normal happy life.

It was a beautiful spring day, the beginning of May and school had just let out for the day. Lori decided to go to Valley Hill to enjoy a little of the early spring sunshine before going home. When she reached the hill, she climbed to a grassy area where she could look down upon the whole town and stretched out with a sigh. A gentle breeze rustled the trees, and the smell of honeysuckle was strong in the air. The sun shone down brightly out of a clear, blue sky. As she lay there listening to the chirping of the birds and the pleasant humming of the bees, she felt blissfully content and drifted into a daze.

The first thing she became aware of was the absolute silence. A hazy fog drifted down shadowing the brilliant sunshine. She sat up abruptly, her heart already speeding up. What had happened to the sun? Where were the birds? Then a sound started in the distance. A soft humming sound that increased to a road and caused the fog to writhe and twist like a living creature. Suddenly, he was standing there. He was tall, very tall, and his hair midnight black. He had a slender build but his most riveting feature were his piercing blue eyes. Now he turned those hypnotic eyes on Lori.

"Do not fear me", he said. "I mean you no harm."

Lori stared in awe for she realized that his lips were not moving, yet she heard the words in her mind.

"You are so beautiful", he whispered, "And I must join with you."

Lori suddenly panicking backed hastily away, but the stranger simply reached out and placed both hands on her waist. Blue fire shot from his hands. Blue light circled her waist like a wreath she became aware of a slow paralysis affecting body. It started at her feet and moved up slowly until the numbness enveloped her entire body. Gently he placed her back on the grassy patch. He smoothed her hair back and whispered.

"I will not hurt you. Do not be afraid."

Then he placed one hand over her forehead and the other cross her stomach. Immediately she was aware of a strange tingling in her belly. Then he placed her hands in the same positions on his body and she gasped as sensation after magnificent sensation passed through her body. She clenched her teeth as feeling exploded inside of her, and then she opened her eyes. Although she could not see his mouth, somehow she knew he was smiling. He then kissed two fingers and placed them on her dry lips.

"You are enchanting," he said. "We have such need of you in our time. I will be back for the child. Protect him from those who would harm him."

Lori, suddenly gaining control again of her body grasped his arm and yelled, "What child? Please, you must tell me who you are and where your from."

"You will know all this in time" again swirling and thick then thinning out into a trail of smoke and, he whispered. Then the fog roared in again swirling and thick then thinning out into a trail of smoke and Lori was left standing alone in the little glade. Had she dreamed it all? Lori was inclined to think so, especially since the sun was every bit as brilliant as it had been before. Nothing had changed in the little glade. The spring noises continued, the sky was blue, no trace of fog but she, Lori herself felt different. She was almost afraid to think about how different, but there was nothing and no one to prove that the episode had happened except in her mind, so she simply picked up her books and walked slowly home.

Days passed and Lori had put the dream or whatever it was out of her mind. Then one morning she woke up nauseous and achey. Her mother checked her over, found her fever less, and decided she must have a bug of some kind. Curiously, only an hour or so later, Lori woke and the sickness disappeared. When the same thing happened two more days in a row, Lori knew. She was pregnant. The time she'd spent with the strange man was an incident she'd forced herself to forget. Now all the strange events came tumbling back to cloud her mind as if happened yesterday.

How could she tell her mom? Who'd believe her strange story? Already her clothing tightened across her expanding waistline. She'd have to tell someone soon. Finally, one evening she told her mother the whole story. Evie was incredulous.

"Honey, that's impossible. You can't become pregnant that way. I'm your mother. You can tell me the truth."

"Mother", Lori replied. "I am telling you the truth. He said he'd be back. I didn't understand, but now I know he meant when the child is born."

"Lori dear, her mother answered as she sat down next to her, "If you slipped up with some boy from the village. I'll understand, but this ridiculous story."

"It's true mother", sniffed Lori. "I know how it sounds but it's true."

Lori continued to school, for graduation loomed ahead and there were only days left. The other students teased her unmercifully. HERE COMES LORI, SPACE MOTHER, they'd yell whenever she walked by. Lori absorbed it all with quiet dignity, and eventually the teasing stopped. Aft the end of June, Lori graduated with honors but the bright, happy future she envisioned was gone. There was no way she could start college in the fall five months pregnant. By the end of the summer Lori looked radiant. The sickness she'd suffered in the early stages disappeared and as the child grew larger, Lori grew prettier. Even her doctor told her she was the healthiest pregnant woman she'd ever seen. Lori was surprisingly quite happy except when one of the villagers snubbed her openly. Though none of them believed her story, the snubbing eventually disappeared entirely. Lori was now free to anticipate the birth of her baby with the same excitement all mothers have.

December arrived with its brisk, cold days, twinkling snowflakes, and all the excitement of Christmas. The Villagers now accepted Lori and he pregnancy, so she shopped happily with two of her friends from school. Working part time during the summer, had earned her a little, so now she eagerly picked out gifts for her family and the baby. Christmas was spent with her friends and family and went fabulously well. Then Lori threw herself into making preparations for the baby.

After much searching, she discovered an antique cradle in one of the little shops in town. She sanded and painted it and then polished it until it glowed. She emptied out her mom's sewing room and painted it a soft yellow. Then she found and old chest in the attic and painted it to match the cradle. She spent two days cutting and pasting to make a Mobile for the baby.

Evie watched her daughter worriedly. If the story she'd told her was true, 1 this stranger would be back to collect the baby and Lori seemed to forget this vital point. Carefully, she broached the subject one wintry afternoon.

"Lori, sweetheart", her mother called. "Could you sit down a minute and talk to me."

"Sure, mother", Lori said as she squeezed her expanded belly into her favorite spot on the couch.

I've watched you lately, Honey. You're becoming so attached to the baby."

"Of course, mother. I love my baby. What did you think? That I wouldn't want it because of its beginning."

"Of course not", Evie replied. "I know my daughter. It's the father, Honey. The father will be back and he will want his child."

"I know, mother", replied Lori. "He can't have it. I eon't give up my baby."

January arrived with a blast. Wind whipped the cold, wet snow into a frenzy. Flakes smacked against the windows making little wet kisses on the pane. Lori waddled her way to the window and sank down heavily on the window seat. She felt a vague ache in the lower part of her back. The baby, which was usually moved continuously was uncharacteristically still. Lori used her elbow to rub a clear spot on the foggy window. Suddenly, she doubled over as an excruciating pain traveled from the small of her back around to her stomach. When it stopped she knew two things immediately. The baby was on its way, and HE was back.

Although Lori prepared for this moment for months, there was still panic in her voice as she turned from the window and yelled, "Mom, mom I think it's time."

Evie came running.

"Oh Honey", she murmured. "I didn't think this would happen for weeks yet. Now sit here and I'll call the doctor."

Lori grasped her mother's arm. "Mom, not only that. He's back. I can feel him. He's out there and he's coming for my baby."

Evie tugged nervously at her short, dark curls. "Well, we'll get you to the hospital and we'll worry about him later."

A cold wet wind burst through the room as suddenly the door opened. A tall, dark figure moved into the room. "I am here," he said.

Lori gasped as another pain caused her to sit down quickly. Evie stared anxiously at the stranger, but she still managed to grab Lori's coat and wrap it around her shoulders. "Come, Honey", she pleaded. "We have to go."

The stranger stepped forward. "No", he said.

Evie gasped. "We have to go. The baby—

"I will take care of her", said the man. "Where is the bedroom?"

"But, but", Evie began.

"Relax", said the man. He lifted Lori as if she were a feather. He glided up the steps, talking calmly to Lori all the way. Over his shoulder, he told Evie, "Bring hot water and clean blankets. She will be fine. I'll see to it."

A short time later Lori lay in bed. The man took off his cape and hat and for the first time, Lori could see him clearly. His hair grew to his collar, dark and luxurious. He was tall and slender. When he smiled at her, twin dimples appeared simultaneously on his face and of course, he had those piercing blue eyes. He placed a slender hand on her forehead and the new pain just starting, stopped immediately.

"Now , he said. I'll tell you about me. I come from your future. A hundred years ahead. Yes, in my time, we have such sexual freedom that the sexual diseases got out of hand. It didn't affect the carrier, but the babies were born sickly and many of them died.

Lori whispered, "But we didn't, didn't—

"No", the man smiled. "We developed that new way to have sex. We feel the same sensations, but since the bodies do not come in contact;: He with each other, we cannot spread disease. And, yes, one can get pregnant.

He placed his hand gently on her stomach. Soon as he removed his hand her head, another pain raged through her middle.

"I know", he said, "The child is the birth position. I can take away the pain, but soon you will feel great pressure. Then the child will come."

"Lori grasped his free hand. "I want to keep my baby", she said. "Who are you that dares to take my baby?"

"In my time I am called Seth, and I did not just want the child. I want you as well."

Lori clutched at his hand and panted, It's time. The baby's coming." At that moment Evie appeared in the doorway bearing a pot of hot water, clean towels, and blankets. Seth leaned forward and placed both hands on Lori's stomach and she panted and pushed the baby out. Evie rushed forward with the towel as a squalling, tiny baby boy pushed head first into the world. Seth placed his hands on the umbilical cord and a little flash of blue light cut it and sealed it in seconds. Then he placed the tiny boy in Lori's waiting arms while Evie collected the afterbirth in old newspapers. "He's beautiful, Honey", she whispered giving Lori a kiss. The baby had a mass of dark hair, and as Lori bent forward to kiss him, he opened his eyes displaying startling blue corneas. His tiny rosebud mouth opened and closed like a little bird, and one tiny puckered fist caught in his mother's long hair.

Much later after Lori had had a well deserved rest, Evie came in and at on the bed.

"Seth said you might have something important to tell me", she whispered smoothing tendrils of hair off Lori's forehead. "How do you feel?'

Lori smiled tiredly. "Like I've been run over by a truck. It wasn't so bad though, thanks to Seth." "Mom", Lori hesitated. "I think I'm going to leave with him. I can't give up the baby and he always wanted me to come with him."

Evie sighed. "I sort of thought this might happen. Are you sure this is really what you want?"

"I really do. He's from many years in our future. The stories he tells me are like a page from one of my books. I'd be living one of my dreams. Except I'd miss you so. Mom and my little sister, Angie.

Evie rose slowly and walked over to the cradle. She patted the sleeping baby gently on his back. "I love you and little Sidney so already. I don't know if I can handle this Lori. Would you be able to return?"

"Seth claims there is danger involved. The possibility of someone coming from his time to ours or vice-versa. That's the reason he uses the fog cover, less danger of anyone seeing him. But if we're very careful, I think we will be able to come back. They chose Seth specifically for this mission, but I don t think they expected him to fall in love."

Evie continued to stand near the baby. Now she was caressing the dark curls. Lori climbed out of bed, walked over and hugged her mom tightly and kissed her cheek.

"Mom, that's not all. We have to leave within the week. I'm sorry", she whispered.

Several days later on a bitterly cold day Seth and Lori said their good-bys and left. Angie and Evie watched from the window as Seth guided his family to the edge of the forest. Minutes later he wrapped his huge cape around them, the fog swirled in and when it cleared, they were gone. Days passed and Evie often looked in the baby's room, Lori had prepared so lovingly. She'd told all the Villagers that Lori's boyfriend had come back for her and the baby, which was almost the truth after all.

One evening she lay awake missing Lori more than ever when she heard some sound coming from the baby's empty room. As she opened the door, wisps of smoke floated out into the hallway. Then she gasped. For the little cradle and set of drawers were gone as well as the Mobile, Lori had worked so hard on. In the middle of the floor lay a piece of engraved wood.

82

It Read:

Dear Mom,

Please don't worry. It's even more wonderful than I dreamed. Inside the wood is a picture of Sidney. Thing's are changing here already so we will be back someday soon.

Love Lori,

ON THE EDGE

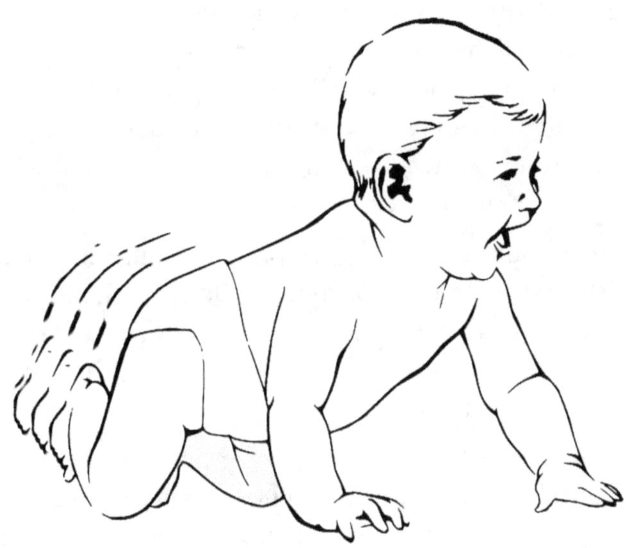

ON THE EDGE

IT WAS THE twenty-ninth day of July, exactly one month before Lynne's baby was due. The women in the office where she worked had been planning for weeks to surprise her with a baby shower. When Lynne left for one of her many bathroom breaks, the women were ready. Rita brought out the cake, Pat piled presents around Lynne's desk, Tabitha dragged in an extra-large box and stood it in the aisle, and Jean rolled in a stroller. When Lynne returned, she was flabbergasted to find her work space transformed into a party.

For the next hour, she unwrapped presents, laughed, cried, ate too much, and then, with Rita's help, took stock of her gifts. She got the usual—two sweater sets, one white and one yellow, two panty sets, five little kimonos, a comb and brush set, a bassinet set, three packages of disposable diapers, and a stroller.

Finally, she gathered her two diaper bags, two panty sets, and four baby outfits, repacked them to be taken home, and opened the big box. There was the gift she most loved, a swinger. It was yellow and green and had a tiny seat with holes for the baby's legs. The swinger needed its legs attached, and there was a key on the side. When set up, it would rock at three different speeds while playing a lullaby to help the baby sleep.

Lynne adored it, but, after promptly packing everything away at home, she stored the swinger in the closet and awaited the baby's birth.

The next four weeks were uneventful. On the morning of September first, Jessica was born at one-ten. She had huge, dark, thickly lashed eyes, soft brown curls on her head, and tiny dimples in her cheeks. Dan and Lynne were in awe of the tiny angel they created.

Several weeks later, Lynne had an extraordinarily hectic day. She was down to her last disposable diaper, and all her cloth diapers were dirty. The sink was filled with many dirty dishes, the vacuum sat on a dirty rug and wasn't touched, and Lynne walked her colicky baby from the kitchen to the living room, but Jessica kept crying. Lynne wanted to scream in frustration.

She swung open the closet door, frantically looking for a diaper, and saw the swinger in the corner.

That would be perfect right now, she thought. Dan even has it all assembled.

She dragged it out with one hand, Jessica balanced in the opposite arm, then set it in the corner of the living room, checked to make sure the batteries were in, and set Jessica in the seat. She strapped Jessica in and turned the key. The swinger swayed in time to a nursery rhyme, and Jessica stopped crying.

Lynne was ecstatic. She finished the housework, washed and dried diapers, and still the baby rocked. When she peeked in later, Jessica was fast asleep. She put her to bed and turned off the swinger, giving it a lovely pat.

"You're a miracle worker," she said.

It creaked a few times before coming to rest, and Lynne thought it sounded like it was saying, *I am. I am. I am.*

She smiled at herself. What an imagination I have, she thought, walking off to finish dinner.

The next day, Dan came home from work early, and Lynne saw something was wrong.

"They're downsizing," he said. "As of today, my job is gone, unless

. .

"Unless what?" Lynne asked.

"There's a branch of the company in California, and they need workers there. The company would send me there and pay me a higher salary if I agreed to a transfer."

Lynne sat down thoughtfully. She and Dan had been married for three years, and they'd found the perfect home the previous year. It was finally beginning to look like a home.

"I know, Honey," Dan said. "We can't afford to lose my salary at this critical time. I know you don't want to give up the house.

"Jessica and I don't want to be separated from you, either.

"Look, I don't want to be separated, but I'll visit. Pennsylvania isn't off the map. The situation is supposed to be temporary. The company's reorganizing, and they expect to have a place open for me here within four months."

They discussed it for hours and finally decided Dan should go. He planned to return for Thanksgiving, and, if no position in his company opened up, he would return within four months and look for a job.

The next week, Lynne washed dishes and wiped away an occasional tear. Dan left early that morning, and she felt vulnerable and lonely. Jessica rocked in the swinger, and, in the mornings silence, she thought she heard words in the swinging rhythm.

You're on the edge. You're on the edge. Dan's gone. Dan's gone. You're on the edge . . .

She was so rattled by it, she ran into the living room to look at the swinger. It rocked harmlessly and played London Bridge as Jessica played with her rattle on the little white tray.

I must miss Dan more than I thought, Lynne thought. *I don't want to go nuts.* She returned to the kitchen to finish her chores.

Several weeks passed, and Lynne continued to use the swinger, because Jessica was so content in it. One morning, when she was extremely busy, she thought she heard more words coming from it.

You're alone, Lynne. You're alone, Lynne.

She shook her head. *I'd better take Jessica out of the house more often.* She glanced at the gloomy piles of dirty snow outside and shook her head. *I'll try to stay a little longer.*

Several days later, she used the swinger to quiet Jessica, who was extremely irritable. Jessica was getting more and more fussy when she wasn't in the swinger.

As Lynne came up the basement steps, she thought she heard, Dan's gone. Dan's gone. I win. I win.

As she reached the top of the steps, the sound lapsed into the nursery rhyme, Twinkle, Twinkle, Little Star. Lynne was so shaken, she snatched Jessica from the swinger and shoved it into the closet, then locked the door.

A few days later, after getting soaked on a nasty, wet October day, Lynne caught a bad cold. She awoke the next morning feeling feverish and miserable, with an aching throat, so she called Susanne, a friend.

Susanne?" she croaked into the receiver, "could you come over to take care of Jessica? She's crying for her morning bottle, and I can't get out of bed"

"Don't worry about a thing," Susanne replied. "I'll be right over. Just unlock the door for me."

Susanne arrived in five minutes. She changed Jessica and fed her a bottle, then, when she slept, made hot lemon tea and toast for Lynne.

As Lynne drank her tea, Susanne sat on the bed.

"I have a proposition for you," Susanne said. "Let me take Jessica home for a day or two. That'll get her away from your germs and give you a chance to rest and recuperate. I brought some soups, a few puddings, and even a casserole you can pop into the oven. You can relax, rest, and watch TV until you're well."

Lynne reluctantly agreed. It would be nice to just lie in bed without having to make formula or change diapers.

The first day and night were uneventful. Other than missing Jessica, Lynne enjoyed her day of solitude and relaxation.

The next day was just as calm, and Lynne felt a lot better. Her fever was gone, and the throat pain diminished, but she was still extremely tired.

She was sound asleep at one o'clock the following morning when someone woke her. She wrapped a robe around her, put on her fuzzy blue slippers, and walked cautiously downstairs to the living room.

At first, there was nothing out of place, then she heard a familiar squeak and turned as a beam of moonlight illuminated a corner of the living room.

There sat the swinger. As Lynne watched, it began to swing, and she thought she heard, *Where's the baby? Where's the baby?*

She felt as if her feet were frozen into place, and a chill went down her spine. She grasped the railing as shocks of terror went through her.

Finally, she moved one foot, then the other. She ran frantically into the kitchen, stumbling over the coffee table. A wave of pain shot up her ankle, but she kept running until she ran into the refrigerator.

In the other room, the chant grew louder.

Where's the baby? Where's the baby?

Lynne grabbed her coat off the hook by the kitchen door and ran out into the cold, dark night. Thankfully, her car keys were in her coat pocket. She fumbled the key into the lock and opened the door. Behind her, a thundering voice called, *Where's the baby? Where's the baby!*

With shaking fingers, she thrust the key into the ignition and turned the switch. The engine caught on the third try, and all sound in the house ceased. Lynne shifted into drive and drove away quickly, but her heartbeat didn't return to normal for two blocks.

She parked in Susanne's driveway and sat in the car until she felt calm enough to ring the doorbell.

When Susanne answered, Lynne fell into her arms, gasping and crying.

"Whoa, Honey," Susanne said. "What's wrong? Do you feel worse? Come in. Sit down, and calm down."

She helped her friend into the house and on the sofa, then bustled about preparing tea. As she set a cup of steaming tea in front of Lynne, Susanne said, "Now, Honey, tell me what's wrong."

"This is going to be hard to believe," Lynne said, trying not to cry. "I think the baby's swinger is haunted."

"Haunted?" Susanne smiled. "Honey, that cold has really gotten to you. You probably had a nightmare from some cold medication. You said that swinger was the next-best thing to a baby-sitter."

"I know." Lynne nervously swallowed some tea. "I believe it talks, and I don't mean nursery rhymes."

Susanne stared at her. "You sound like you're serious."

"I am. I locked it in the closet, and tonight, it woke me! It was sitting in the corner of the living room, yelling, 'Where's the baby?'"

"Tell you what. We'll go to bed, get a good night's sleep, then tomorrow, we'll go to your house and look at the swinger. I'll even stay a few nights and see what happens. If it still upsets you, we'll get rid of it."

Lynne agreed, but it was a long time before she fell asleep that night.

The next morning, they returned in Susanne's car, and Susanne led the way into the house. A bunch of pot holders and refrigerator magnets lay on the kitchen floor, which must've fallen when Lynne ran into it. The coffee table stood lopsided in the middle of the floor, but the swinger wasn't in sight.

Lynne stood there and gasped.

Susanne walked to the closet, opened the door, and saw the swinger in its box, just as Lynne had packed it. Nothing was out of place. Susanne looked at her friend sympathetically as she sat down with her baby.

"Maybe it was a fantastically realistic nightmare," Susanne suggested.

"I don't think so." Lynne put Jessica into her crib in the bedroom.

That night, Lynne and Susanne sat eating popcorn and watching a movie, when suddenly, Susanne said, "Look, I know you're afraid of it, but, if you keep it locked up and don't face your fears, how will we know if anything's wrong with it?"

"All right, but you get it out. I won't touch it."

Susanne set it up and looked it over. It seemed harmless enough. She turned on the switch, and it moved back and forth, playing Mary Had a Little Lamb.

Jessica squirmed in Lynne's arms, then crawled to the swinger and whined for Susanne to lift her in.

"I don't know," Lynne said in concern.

"Oh, Lynne, it seems harmless." Susanne lifted Jessica into the seat. She giggled and cooed, and the swinger rocked and played.

Susanne stayed in Lynne's house for one week. When she wasn't at work, she and Lynne baked cookies, did each other's hair, watched old movies, and ate. Susanne loved to cook, and she cooked enough meals to last Lynne a month, wrapping them and freezing them for Lynne to thaw later.

During that time, the swinger performed as it should. Jessica seemed entranced by it, which worried Lynne, but Susanne didn't see anything unusual happening.

"You told me that night you were so scared, it called for the baby," Susanne said. "The only way to test that is to take the baby away. Why don't you stay at my house for a week? If nothing unusual happens, we can agree it's safe. If you still feel uneasy, we can trash it."

Lynne was skeptical but agreed to try the plan. She packed enough clothing to last her and Jessica a week, then drove off. She called Dan to tell him she was visiting Susanne for the week, then took Jessica to the library.

After studying several books on witchcraft, Lynne returned to Susanne's house convinced someone had put a spell on the swinger. When Susanne returned from work, Lynne explained her theory.

"You could be right," Susanne said. "There were two big boxes in the storage room the day of the shower. The other was for Angela. Her shower was held the next day."

"Who'd want to give her a haunted swinger?"

"Who brought it out?"

"Tabitha."

"That's right. She was the one who rushed to it. I'll bet she mixed then' up. She wanted yours to go to Angela. You know she hates her."

"But if she hates Angela so much, what is it doing to my baby?" Lynne whispered.

"I don't know, but Jessica seems fine. We really don't know if there anything wrong with it at all. Let's wait and see."

"I know," Lynne whispered.

The first day they spent at Susanne's house, she showed Lynne some of the items she was making for Christmas. She worked in ceramics, creating beautiful pieces for her shop downtown. There was a kiln in the cellar, and, on many nights, Susanne stayed up all night firing her creations. There were all kinds of ceramics on the shelves in different stages of completion.

Lynne saw canister sets waiting for final glazing, dozens of little animals, bowls, ashtrays, music boxes, and several small lamps. She held onto Jessica tightly as they passed shelves of delicate pottery, then she stopped.

"This is beautiful. Can I see it?"

It was a tiny carousel with three tiny horses on it. They sat on a base which would contain a music box, and the horses would turn with the music. It was a dismal gray at the moment, but Lynne still loved it.

"If you really like that one, why don't you work on it while you're here?" Susanne suggested. "I'll tell you what to do. It'll be beautiful when it's finished. You could give it to Jessica for Christmas. It doesn't look like much now, but with some cleaning, paint, and a music box, it'll be exquisite."

"You know what, Suze? I just might work on it. It would be a nice thing for Jessica. How much do you want for it?"

"Not a cent. It'll be my gift. I'll show you how to clean it tonight, then I'll fire it, because it's hard to paint when it's not bisque, even though it can be done. It'll look good either way, and working on it might take your mind off your other problems."

True to her word, Suze showed Lynne how to clean the delicate horses without breaking off their feet, then she gave Lynne an array of paints to choose from and helped her select a music box. The tune she chose was *It's a Small World After All,* and she was very pleased as her creation evolved.

Over the next two days, Lynne became so absorbed in working on the carousel, she almost forgot why she was in Susanne's house, but the thought remained in the back of her mind like a dark cloud.

Besides being a connoisseur of ceramics, Susanne was an excellent homemaker. Lynne often wondered how someone with light-brown, bobbed hair and tailored clothes, especially pants, could be so domestic. Susanne was a wonderful cook, her house was immaculate, and there were touches of creativity in every room.

With Jessica, Susanne was the perfect mother. She had a lot of patience and invented little games to keep the child entertained for hours. Lynne, with her long, flowing, dark hair and frilly, ruffled clothes, hated housework but doted on Jessica. That made it all worthwhile. Susanne had a light-hearted attitude and helped her friend through another crisis.

By Saturday, Lynne and Jessica were enjoying the backyard snowball fights and other entertainments Suze created so much, they were reluctant to return home. Nothing unusual had happened during their stay, so Lynn, decided to junk the swinger and forget it. She'd have to make up a story to explain its disappearance to Dan. For some reason, she didn't want him to know of any trouble with the swinger.

Later that night, Suze and Lynne were popping corn and drinking Pepsi in the kitchen. They rented two good movies to watch and bought Jessica some plastic blocks to play with. The two women worked in the kitchen, giggling like two teenagers. They tried to make smores, but they ended up melting the chocolate and dripping marshmallow over the stove.

Jessica played on the living room floor with her new block, chuckling to herself.

"I'll clean up this mess before it sticks," Suze said. "You take the drinks and popcorn in. I'll be right there."

Lynne was still giggling as she carried the huge bowl of popcorn in one hand and balanced their drinks in the other. Then her laughter turned to a scream, and drinks and popcorn flew everywhere as she covered her eyes with her hands.

When she took them away, it was still there—the hated swinger had appeared in the house, and Jessica sat in it, chortling with glee.

"Good God, Lynne, what's wrong?" Suze ran into the room and stopped. "Oh, my God! It's here."

Lynne shook off her paralysis and snatched her baby to safe. The little seat swung back and forth, and a soft voice said, *No, no, no, no.*

"Lynne, take the baby to . . . ." Suze grabbed a piece of paper and write, *Rita's.* "Then come back here and help me. We have to destroy this thing."

"But I don't want. . . ."

"You have to help me. It won't just disappear. You know that. I think I know what to do, now go!"

Lynne ran outside, got in Suze's car, and drove off. Suze stood in the living room and stared at the motionless swinger.

She walked toward it slowly, then warily inspected it, looking on the back, front, and sides. Then she carefully turned it upside down and saw faint writing encircled by an inverted star.

Sit the baby in this seat,

And it will grow with Satan's heat.

"Oh, no," she whispered. "We have to get rid of this thing."

She dragged it into the yard as far from the house as she could get.

Lynne reached Rita's house still in a panic, the composed herself for Jessica's sake. She left Suze's so fast, the baby was wrapped in a single blanket, while all she wore were jeans and a sweater.

She knocked on Rita's door and gasped in the icy wind.

"My God," Rita said, opening the door, "it's Lynne and Jessica. What are you doing out in this weather Come in. What happened?"

"Oh, Rita! Suze and I were popping popcorn. We forgot about it, and the pot caught on fire. We put out the fire, but the house is filled with smoke, so I wanted to get Jessica out of it until we cleaned up. Can you watch her awhile?"

"Why sure. I'll be glad to watch the little angel. Are you sure you can't stay for a piece of cake? I was just having a snack."

"I can't stay right now. I have to help Suze, but I'll be back as soon as we're done cleaning up. Here are some diapers, and these two bottles of milk should last until I get back. She's tired, so she'll probably fall asleep as soon as she has her milk." She kissed Jessica. "I'll be back soon, Honey."

She'll be fine, Lynne." Rita smiled. "I'll let Timmy entertain her awhile, then she'll be ready for warm milk and a nap."

"OK. I won't be too long." She left feeling sad but reached Suze's house quickly.

She found Suze in the backyard, digging in the ground. The swinger sat in the middle of a pile of dirt.

"Have you gone nuts?" Lynne asked.

"No," Suze panted, still digging. "I'm digging a five-pointed star with the evil spirits away. I don't point facing away from the house to drive think the thing can leave the star, but we have to hurry. Go round up some things for me from the house."

"All right. What do you need?"

"A brass bowl filled with salt water, then some gasoline and matches. We're burning this thing."

Lynne left and came back a few minutes later. "All right. I have the stuff. Now what?"

Suze dropped the shovel and ran to Lynne. "OK. Set the bowl of water in the star with the swinger and say this verse with me. We have to say it three times. Wicked spirits touch not me nor mine, thy power I drain into this brine. When we finish the third time, we light it."

"Are you sure you know what you're doing?"

"No, but we have to do something! I'll make sure it stays in the star when you light it."

The wind rose, and flakes of snow began to fall. Lynne grabbed the gas can and poured it over the swinger.

"OK," Suze said. "Hurry up and light it! Then say the verse with me. Hurry!"

Lynne glanced up and saw why Suze was so worried. Huge clouds scudded across the sky, and the wind keened an eerie wail. Every piece of debris on the ground whirled as if caught in a tornado. Everywhere else up and down the street it was twilight, but Suze's backyard was pitch black.

Lynne's fingers trembled as she tried to light the match. Three times, the tiny flame blew out before she got it to the swinger. Finally, with a loud whoosh, the swinger ignited, and flames shot into the sky.

"Now say the verse with me!"

"Look!" Lynne pointed.

The swinger jiggled up and down within the star, and steam rose from the bowl sitting beside it.

"Hurry, Lynne!" Suze shouted over the wind.

They chanted as loudly as they could, screaming to be heard over the rising wind and hissing sound of water.

"Wicked spirits touch not me nor mine, thy power I drain into this brine!" they shouted three times.

A cloud of whirling snow came out of the sky, and pellets of hail fell. The trees in Suze's backyard bent almost to the ground as the wind shrieked louder and louder. Streaks of lightning flashed overhead as the two women cowered from the vicious hail.

The swinger, even though completely engulfed in flames, fell apart, shaking itself to pieces within the star. From it came a low, "Nooo!" that rose in volume until it made Suze and Lynne cry in pain.

Suze's backyard was an oasis of hell, then all sound stopped. The snow and hail vanished as suddenly as they began.

Lynne and Suze looked around and saw that all that remained of the swinger was ashes. Lynne was shaking, and Suze had tears in her eyes. They gravely swept up the ashes and placed them in the empty bowl, then covered it, took it to the church graveyard, and buried it. Neither woman spoke, as if the last shriek tore away their voices.

Finally, Lynne said, "I'd better get the baby."

"Yes. Get Jessica."

As Lynne drove off, Suze started covering the trench she dug in the backyard.

Jessica was asleep when Lynne arrived, and she remained asleep throughout the drive home. Lynne tucked her into bed, then she and Suze slept, too, very subdued after the horror and excitement of the night.

Before going to bed, Suze hugged Lynne. "Don't worry, Hon. It's all over. It's gone forever."

"I hope so," Lynne replied in a wan, lifeless voice.

Early the next morning, Lynne and Jessica returned home. The first thing Lynne did was destroy the box the swinger came in, then she tried to forget the horror of that Saturday night.

Suze went on with her life, too. Strangely enough, the two women didn't visit each other for several weeks. Lynne understood why—they shared the secret of that horrible night even though they vowed never to mention it again.

One day, Suze was working in her basement and found the carousel Lynne left. She decided to finish it for her and give it to Jessica for Christmas.

Over the next few weeks, Lynne watched Jessica carefully, but the little girl seemed perfectly normal. She played with her toys, and her sweet, loving nature returned. If she missed the swinger, she gave no sign. Lynne wondered if she should take Jessica to the doctor, but what would she tell the doctor to look for?

Besides, she thought, *who would believe me?*

Thanksgiving arrived, and Lynne prepared a huge dinner. She invited Suze and her current boyfriend, and Rita and her family to celebrate Dan's return home.

Everyone arrived simultaneously, and Suze brought two homemade pumpkin pies, while Rita brought a cranberry salad.

The dinner was a big success, with everyone eating too much. Afterward the women sat and talked while the men watched football. The children' played with a huge rubber ball on Lynne's living room carpet.

When Rita took Timmy to the bathroom, Suze leaned over to Lynne and whispered, "Jessica looks fine."

"Yes," Lynne whispered back. "She seems OK."

Rita returned with Timmy.

Eventually, the football game ended, and the guests left, praising Lynne's cooking as they went.

Dan heated up leftovers in the kitchen for a snack. "Honey, I've got good news."

"What is it? We haven't had much time to ourselves today."

"For starters, I'm not going back to California. The company finished reorganizing, and they've got a job for me here. It's better than my old one."

"Oh, that's wonderful! You don't know how glad I am to hear that."

He smiled. "It looks like our problems are over."

"I think so." She hugged him. "I believe you're right."

After that happy evening, Lynne was busy shopping for Christmas presents, baking goodies, and picking a tree with Dan. In the evenings, she and Dan spent hours playing with Jessica, who soon learned how to stand. She was at the stage where everything fascinated her, and she stared at the bright, glittery ornaments on the tree, grabbing for anything within reach with her little chubby hand.

Lynne lavished a lot of love on her daughter, having felt she almost lost her.

Christmas day was bright and clear, with just a stray flake floating in the clear air. After dinner, Lynne and Dan enjoyed the afterglow of

Christmas. The lights on the tree twinkled and the opened presents lay under the tree. Lynne's parents watched a parade on TV.

The doorbell rang, and Lynne answered to find Suze with Ted, her boyfriend.

"I can stay for only a minute," Suze said, "but I wanted to make sure Jessica got this." She handed Lynne a gaily wrapped package. "And this is for you and Dan." She handed her another box. "The one for Jessica is special."

"Come in, Ted," Lynne said, smiling, "and have some Christmas cheer. Suze, you can help me give this to Jessica."

Jessica sat on the floor beside the tree, playing with a toy lawnmower. Whenever she moved it, swirls of colors moved in a circle on the toy, changing designs as they turned.

"Hi, Jessie," Lynne called. "Look what Aunt Suze brought you." She held out the brightly wrapped package, then helped Jessica remove the paper.

"Oh, Suze!" Lynne said. "You finished it!"

It was the carousel. Three tiny horses pranced around the platform, one blue, one pink, and one yellow, done in soft pastels. The little top moved separately from the horses, like a merry-go-round. On the side was a tiny key to wind the music box.

"Look, Jessie," Lynne said. "Isn't it pretty?"

Jessie held the music box in a chubby hand, and suddenly, the little horses turned, and the music box played, *It's a Small World After All.*

"That's cute." Suze laughed. "When did you wind it?"

"I didn't."

They looked at Jessica, who was giggling. Her dark-brown eyes suddenly had a strange yellowish glow, and the little carousel spun faster and faster, the tune playing gaily on and on.

OUT LIKE A LION

It was the third day of March, when Tina flipped the calendar over, a couple of days behind as she was with everything lately. It was a bright, sunny day with a touch of spring in the air, but with enough of a nip to let one know that winter hadn't left yet. She fussed with her hair for a few minutes and then she turned and looked, really, really, looked at the calendar. It was a cat calendar which she had saved up box tops to get. And usually the cats pictured were cottony little balls of fluff chat made one go all soft inside, but the cat pictured for March was a cruel looking, tawny colored short hair. It was gaunt, yet wiry but it was the eyes that really made a shiver run down her back. They were green, but a silverish, wild kind of green and they glittered. No matter where she stood in the room, the eyes seemed to be watching her with a fiendish type of glee. My God, I must be losing my mind she thought, and then she rushed out of the room realizing she was almost late for work. She was so busy that day, that she completely forgot the calendar incident until she returned home.

That night she looked at the calendar again as she was preparing for bed and still the unusual cat made her feel uneasy. Why not just rip the page off if it bothers you, she reasoned. Because it's only the third of March, and I'm a little embarrassed to be so afraid of a colored picture on a page, she thought. Then she called Tiger, her car, who curled up beside her and they both fell asleep.

Two weeks passed uneventfully except that she still felt nervous about the picture on the calendar, but now it had become a principle with her to see if she could wait it out until April, when she could legally throw away the page and forget about it. Another unusual thing that had occurred since this unique calendar page, was that Tiger her lovable cat, would no longer sleep or even come into the room, no matter how much she coaxed her. Oh well, thought Tina, once March is over, and I can legally destroy that picture, everything will be all right again.

The next day when Tina looked at the picture, her heart dropped into the pit of her stomach. The cat on the calendar seemed to be changing positions and the eyes focused on her with malevolent evil. This is she thought. I'm going to destroy this page right now. But a strange thing happened when her fingers touched the calendar. She tugged and she pulled, and struggled, but the page would not rip off. Tina was astonished. Was she going crazy? Then she tried to take the whole calendar off the wall, but it was hot to the touch. She could not remove it, somehow she knew she would be able to remove it when March ended, but now nothing would it off before then. Tina didn't understand this strange set of circumstances, but she was compelled to end the problem in the only logical way she could, wait for the month to end.

The next night she heard or thought she heard a cat cry, a menacing, hideous, yowel but Tiger hadn't slept in her room in two weeks and besides she had never heard Tiger cry like that in her entire life. But now there only six more days left in March, and Tina knew with the ending of the month, her fear and foreboding of the calendar would be gone. I just might throw the whole darn thing in the trash, she thought.

Five more days to go she breathed, when she got out of bed the next morning. She looked at the calendar and the cat actually seemed to be smiling at her. It's lips were lifted in a diabolic, half sneer, half smile, and Tina was terrified. She threw her bathrobe over the picture, but she could still see it in her mind and though she was trembling she whispered, "You're not going to win. You've got four more days and you are gone forever.

March thirty-first finally arrived, and Tina was elated. Things had gone exceptionally well at work that day, and tonight she could rip that evil picture off her calendar, and her days of fear would be over. She had really missed Tiger's presence by her side these last few weeks. And so tonight to celebrate the destroying of the calendar, she coaxed Tiger into her room with a bit of hamburger and then placed Tiger in her bed when he had finished eating. Tiger seemed a little apprehensive at first, but after snuggling up next to Tina, he curled up and went right to sleep. Tina and Tiger were both sleeping soundly when at 11:59 A.M., she heard a horrible shriek and then a hissing sound close to her ear. Tina screamed and fumbled for the light switch with trembling hands, and then she stared anxiously at the calendar. : "Oh no," she whispered as tears streamed down her face, for on the picture where that evil cat had been was her beloved gentle Tiger, and lying beside her on the bed, ghoulishly smiling up into her eyes was the wicked, evil cat from the calendar.

REPLACED

arah glanced at her watch again, and then spurted even faster up the Mall. Zig zagging though the lunch hour crowd, she went ducking head on collisions at every turn. A few people detached themselves from their conversations to stare at her curiously. However, the hot dog man in front of Revco Drugs plopped a steaming dog into a bun, then just smiled at her. He was used to seeing her make this run every day. Most people just ignored her though, until she crashed headlong into a red hair woman wearing dark glasses. The woman was holding the leash of a collie, which Sarah now realized was a seeing eye dog. Backing up quickly, Sarah yelled,

"I'm sorry, I'm sorry, I'm just so late," and continued running up the street.

She only glanced back once as she crossed the street and saw the woman going into a store. Good, she thought, at least she hadn't knocked her over. Now the building loomed ahead that she was sprinting to. Should she try to sneak in the front entrance which would save her time or go in the proper coworkers entrance which would extend her lateness by ten minutes.

Sarah chose the front. Now how to get in that way without any of the workers in the store seeing her. Noticing a bunch of teenagers just entering, Sarah thrust herself into the middle of them and stayed there until she reached the first escalator. The steps ascended slowly caterpillar like. Almost there, she thought. She looked around again. Had anyone noticed her? She didn't think so. She felt safe. But then she'd felt safe the other time too when she'd been hauled into Mr. Martin's office seconds after she returned.

"Mrs. Brown, do you know why you were told to see me?" Devon Martin asked before she had even sat down.

"No, I don't think I do," Sarah answered, trying not to wiggle her feet. She always wiggled her feet when she was nervous.

"Well, I'll enlighten you immediately," he said closing the door behind her.

"Your fellow coworkers have observed you using the customer entrance on your lunch hour. That is not permitted."

"But I only"—Sarah started.

"And," he continued, freezing her with a furious frown, "In a period of twenty-one days you have been late a total of fifth teen times. That will not be tolerated. Now, Mrs. Brown I'm going to give you a probationary period of two weeks and if you are late during that period, I will have to initiate disciplinary action."

Sarah swallowed nervously. "You're not going to can me are you?"

"Look, Mrs. Brown. Everyone else in your office can abide by the rules. If you want to remain part of this company, you will have to learn to conform."

"I promise I'll try but what if I have some emergency and it happens again."

"Then," said Mr. Brown, "You will be given a week off without pay and if when you return you have some "emergency" again, you will be replaced."

Now here she was trying to sneak in ten minutes delinquent on her lunch hour again.

"Please," she whispered. "Please don't let anyone see me. I need this job. With two kids depending on me I can't afford a week off without pay." She glanced down the escalator. Was anyone watching her? That woman by the mirror seemed to be looking her way. She hoped not. The trick was to get back to her desk without being noticed. Through the store, she sprinted to the office entrance. Oh, my goodness, she thought. My jacket, I forgot, my jacket. Quickly she pulled it off and stuffed it in her purse. Let everyone wonder why she carried a basket sized purse. She knew why. She felt like a salmon fighting her way upstream as she struggled through the crowds to her destination.

Finally, the entrance loomed ahead and she was in luck, the receptionist was not at her desk. She edged into the office sneakily. Now if she could make it into the file room without anyone seeing her, then maybe she could grab some mimeograph paper and pretend she'd been making copies. So far so good. She grabbed up a pile of blank sheets and walked to the office entrance. Almost home free. Just a few more steps—Oh no!! Miss Sanders just ahead in the doorway. "Hello, Mrs. Brown. You certainly are speedy today. Why just five minutes ago, I had you sorting mail for me. Have you finished that already?"

Sarah responded, "No Miss Sanders. I'm not that fast. I just wanted to get these copies made while the copy machine was available. I'll get right back to that mail."

"You know, Sarah, I wanted to tell you how glad I am you took Mr. Martin's advice and have been on time for the last two weeks. Your work has improved too."

"Why, thank you Miss Sanders," Sarah said as she continued on to her seat.

Sure enough, three piles of freshly sorted mail sat in near rows across her desk. Who had done it? Certainly not her. And she'd been late three times last week. She'd hoped Miss Sanders was covering for her. There were other things that bothered her too, now that she thought about it. Her top drawer, the one she tossed everything into, her own private dump was as neat as a pin. Pencils and pens were all lined up in rows like little soldiers. Erasers, paper clips, everything sat in its own special compartment. Paper had its own slot also, neatly stacked.

As she looked up, Miss Sanders approached with another armful of mail.

"Great," she said, Here's another pile to sort. I'll take the finished piles."

For the rest of the afternoon, Sarah was kept too busy to wonder about the strange happenings, but when she reached home that evening, it started all over again.

She planned spaghetti and meatballs for supper, so on the way home she stopped and bought the ingredients. Now she stood in her bedroom changing out of her work clothes as the children played in the yard. What a strange day it had been. She'd expected to be given a week off without pay. Instead, she'd been commended for doing an excellent job.

Returning from her shower, the tantalizing smell, garlic and tomatoes sent her running down the steps. Then she stopped in utter shock. The table was set for the three of them, a huge bouquet of flowers in the center. Golden, crusty garlic bread, slightly warm, sat on a huge platter. A large bowl of spaghetti sat on the table next to a perfectly made salad, and on the stove boiling away in a delicious sauce were the meatballs. But the children were still outside. She could hear them laughing as they bounced a basketball. Who had prepared the meal? Sarah stood puzzling this as Rachel and Robbie came running in.

"Mom, what smells so good?" yelled Robbie.

"Yeah, Mom, we could smell it outside," said Rachel. "Oh, she stopped short. "Robbie, look Mom set the table."

"Wow! said Robbie. Is this a special occasion, Mom?"

Sarah sat down shakily. It wouldn't do for her to go stark raving mad in front of her children.

"Mom, are you O.K.? asked Rachel. "You look kind of funny."

"I'm all right, Honey, she whispered. "Just a little tired tonight. Now go wash up. As you can see everything is ready.'

While they were gone Sarah visibly pulled herself together. Someone must be playing a joke on her. They'd come in cooked the meal and left. The door was left open for the children. One of her oddball friends was just playing a trick. Any minute they'd bust in, laugh with her, and then invite themselves to supper. Rachel and Robbie returned to dinner and soon they were all eating dinner which was delicious and no one burst through the door proclaiming a joke.

"Mom," Rachel ladled more salad on her plate. "How come? We never sit at the table and eat, but it is kind of nice, you know."

"Yeah, Mom," chimed in Robbie. "We always eat in front of the T.V. doing our homework."

"Well tonight I thought we'd eat like a civilized family," said Sarah with a shaky smile.

Rachel ate another meatball. "Mom, why do you keep watching the door?"

Sarah swallowed nervously. All this good food. It tasted like straw in her mouth . . . And no one was coming to laugh at the huge joke they played on her. Sarah was close to hysteria but she only smiled at Rachel and said, "Honey I was expecting a package. That's all. I thought it might come tonight."

"Oh, O.K. Mom. It was a great dinner, but I have two pages of Math to do. Leave the dishes though. Robbie and I will do them later. After all you cooked that great meal."

Then off she went to finish her homework, and Robbie went to engage the Play Station. Sarah cleared the table, but even as she worked her brain whirled in confusion. What was happening to her? Maybe she was losing her mind. The weird thing about these recent happenings was that things were being done which she always wanted to do, but never seemed to have the time to do. She waned to be efficient at work, but something always slowed her down, she wanted to be on time but something always happened to trip her up, she enjoyed having dinner with the children at the table but it always seemed like there was never enough time. Now something was living her life the way she wanted to but couldn't.

Later while the children washed the dishes, Sarah did a quick straighten up job on the house. Then she laid out an outfit for tomorrow and one for Robbie. Every second she saved in the morning counted and she knew no matter what was happening, she couldn't take a chance on being late again. Finally, she set all the clocks in the house ahead ten minutes.

Even as she worked Sarah kept glancing over her shoulder not knowing what she feared, but when she cleaned the bathtub, she caught herself staring at her reflection in the mirror for quite a while.

Two weeks passed uneventfully though Sarah made a special effort to be more responsible in all areas of her life. Then one evening, Sarah remained in the store after work. She needed a new outfit and hadn't bought one in over a year. To be efficient, one must look efficient was Miss Sanders motto. Even as she walked from counter to counter, Sarah felt a vague apprehension which kept growing. Finally, at six o'clock she gave up. Nothing she tried on looked right. She'd have to bring Rachel along. Rachel had such excellent taste and more knowledge of the changing styles then she did. When she reached home, Sarah was startled to find the house dark and Rachel and Robbie nowhere in sight. Unlocking the kitchen door Sarah entered the silent house her anxiety growing. Where could they be? Sarah glanced out the back window. Nothing. She moved through the kitchen again and then checked the refrigerator door for a note. No note. As her eyes moved to the old cat calendar right over the refrigerator, she gasped. Oh no!! She couldn't have forgotten Robbie's first track meet. But there written across the today's date in huge red letters DON'T FORGET, MOM, ROBBIE'S TRACK MEET. The Maybe I can get there she thought frantically, and then saw the clock. It was no use. The meet would be over by now They were probably on their way home. Robbie would be so hurt and what had she been doing. Roaming through a store and it had all been a total waste of time. She sat down wearily at the kitchen table.

"Oh God," she whispered. "Please let Robbie forgive me."

Outside, the sound of a truck pulling up drew her attention. She hurried to the window. No, not a truck, a brown and black Ford blazer. Sarah watched the door open and Rachel step out laughing.

"You did great, Robbie," She was saying.

Robbie appeared next with a huge smile on his face and then –

"Oh, No," Sarah whispered. "It can't be!!!!" Her knees buckled, but the window seat held her in place so she was forced to watch a duplicate of herself exit the van.

"So long, Tom," the duplicate Sarah yelled. "Thanks for the ride home."

"Anytime Sarah," Tom yelled back as he drove off. Now she wrapped her arms around Rachel's waist and patted Robbie's head who was jumping and cheering his way up the walk.

"Mom, I'm so glad you came," Rachel was saying. "You know how you always forget everything. Look how happy you've made Robbie."

Now, halfway to the door, the duplicate Sarah raised her head and looked straight at the window where Sarah lay shaking and crying on the window seat. She looks just like me thought Sarah, everything an exact duplicate, but not the eyes. She shuddered. The eyes are not human. Sarah watched as she leaned down and whispered something to Rachel. Rachel nodded and then she disappeared around the back of the house. Stumbling and crying Sarah struggled to the back of the house. She had to see where she went, but when Sarah reached the back window, all she saw were the usual toys scattered about the yard and the worn-down grass. The children were entering the front door laughing and talking. I can't let them find me like this, thought Sarah. Up the steps she stumbled into the bathroom locking the door behind her. Her whole body trembled as she collapsed on the floor. Over and over her mind shouted No, No. Her heartbeat thundered double time and she gasped for air. Suddenly she remembered the pills. She crawled to the medicine cabinet snatching the door open, keeping her eyes averted from her reflection. Thankfully she clutched the bottle of Zanax and dry swallowed a pill as fast as she was able. She hadn't needed them in a year. She hoped they still worked. Slowly her heart returned to normal and she became aware of Rachel calling her.

"Honey, I'm up here. I'll be down in a few minutes," she called back.

"O.K. Mom," said Rachel. "You told us you were getting from the garage. You must have super speed to get up there so fast. Robbie and I will eat these sandwiches you made. They look delicious."

Sandwiches? Sarah's muddled mind was closing down. I didn't your any sandwiches. I have to get myself together. I must talk to the children and with that thought, Sarah went downstairs. Robbie sat holding the two first place medals he'd won and chatting with Rachel. When they saw their mother, Rachel called, "Mom, what do you think of your only son now. Two first places, the long jump and the triple jump."

Sarah knelt down beside Robbie, put her arms around him and hugged him tightly.

"I'm so proud of you," she said. My handsome, talented boy. I wish I could have seen it."

"Mom, you did see it. I could hear you cheering for me."

Sarah stared at the floor, her eyes filling with tears, "It wasn't me Robbie. I was sitting right here in our kitchen, crying because I'd disappointed you, again."

Rachel moved closer and sat down by her mother, "Mom, are you serious?" she asked.

Sarah nodded. "I watched you through the window. You were both so happy but that woman you were with is an impostor."

"Mom, it was you," Rachel said quietly.

"Really, Rachel," Sarah faced her with red rimmed eyes. "Did you really notice no difference at all, because it's trying to take my place and I think she may be succeeding." Rachel stared at her. Suddenly she said, "Robbie, wait. Remember when she bought you that ice cream cone?"

"Yeah, I remember," mumbled Robbie.

"You know how Mom always says "Sweets for the sweet and lemons for the sour." She didn't say it, and she knew we were waiting for her to say something but she didn't know what she was supposed to say."

Sarah interjected, "as if she hadn't been programmed yet?'

"I guess so, Mom." Rachel hugged her. "What are we going to do? We can't tell her from you."

Robbie reached over and grabbed his mother's hand. "Mom, is this the reason you've been acting so weird, lately?"

"Yes, Robbie, can you forgive me for missing your track meet? I promise it will never happen again."

"Sure, Mom, It's O.K."

"No, Robbie, It's not O.K. and I understand that now. In a way I think this has happened because I haven't been the proper Mom both of you need."

"Mom, that's silly," said Rachel.

"Your perfect."

"No Rachel, I'm far from perfect, but I'm going to try to do better. You see, she moves in whenever I slip up and there aren't going to be any more slip ups, not if I can help it." Sarah squared her shoulders. "Now let's all nave a snack and go to bed. We have a big day ahead of us tomorrow and we're going to make it a good one."

Gradually the last traces of winter disappeared, and spring awakened in the world. Sarah's life seemed to be almost perfect. At work, she received a raise from Miss Sanders for a job well done. At home she and the children achieved a glorious rapport with each other. There were no more forgotten track trips and every night the family sat around the dinner table and discussed the day's activities. And no sign of the impostor. Sarah dared to wish it had gone back to whatever hell it came from.

One evening Rachel had gone shopping with friends and Robbie, to a baseball game with several of his pals. An unfamiliar blue Toyota pulled into the driveway. Just as Sarah reached the door, Tom stepped out of the car. When the doorbell rang, Sarah opened the door reluctantly.

"I know, I know," Tom said as he pulled off his cap. "I should've called, but I just got back in town, and I wanted to see the kids right away."

"Well, Tom, I see you haven't changed much. Disorganized as usual. You should've called first. Both Robbie and Rachel are out with their friends. Are you just passing through?"

"Sorry to disappoint you, Honey, but I'm back for good. Don't worry though. I'll stay out of your hair. Just would like to visit the kids. By the way, I'd like to take them out tomorrow night to Pizza Palace and then maybe a movie. Is that all right with you?"

"Tom," Sarah answered.

"You know I have no objection to you seeing the kids anytime you want. They may be a little miffed, however seeing as how you ignored their birthdays last year."

'Sarah," Tom retorted. "Look, you have a right to be angry and so do the kids, but I told you I've changed. I never would've left anyway if you had given me some hope of us getting back together."

"That's not even in the cards, Tom but I will tell the children to be ready tomorrow. You'll be here at what time?"

"Seven sharp." Tom smiled. "Sarah, I'll say it again. I'm sorry about that girl. It only happened twice. She meant nothing to me."

Just having him say the words caused Sarah to flinch at remembered pain. Angrily she replied, "Tom, I don't want to go into that again. The children will be ready. Good night!! Then she firmly closed the door. When Rachel and Robbie returned, and were told about their father's invitation, they were absolutely thrilled. Sarah watched them dance around the living room thinking how quickly they'd forgotten the disappointments of the past.

Rachel suddenly stopped in the middle of a turn. "Mom," she yelled. "Are you coming too?"

"Yes, Mom, are you?" chimed in Robbie.

"No, Honey, I'm not going. I find your Daddy and I get along much better when we're apart."

"Oh, Mom," Robbie started.

But Rachel said, "Mom's right, Robbie. It's best this way. Now don't be a pest." The next evening Tom arrived right on time. After everyone left, Sarah got out the movie she'd rented and a Kentucky Fried Chicken dinner for one. Then she grabbed a tall glass of iced tea from the refrigerator and sat down to enjoy her evening. Funny, she thought as she flicked on the VCR, I could have sworn there was only a little tea left but the pitcher was full. Rachel must've made some more. Sarah sighed happily as she flicked on her favorite movie "Ghost".

Sarah nibbled on a piece of chicken. Thank goodness that awful experience that started in January was finally starting to fade from her mind. But now Sarah mused was she really safe or was that thing just waiting for her to foul up again, like, like, (Sarah gasped) like maybe tonight. Tom and the children, out there alone, the perfect opportunity for her to slip in.

"No," Sarah whispered. "No, she's gone!! She wouldn't dare come back!!" Sarah stared at the screen. In the movie, the typical criminal type had just been killed by a car, his dead self still lying in the street. Now his soul (the duplicate him) was being dragged away by some evil dark figures from the underground. Sarah shuddered. Is that what would happen to her if she ever met up with her duplicate?

Sarah ate a piece of roll. "How many times did she show up anyway?" thought Sarah. Let's see, there was the day I was late at lunch time, and when I missed Robbie's track meet, and the day the dinner was ready, just three times. No, wait, she thought. Miss Sanders never missed me the week I was late three times. She must've taken my place. That would make six times, and if she shows up tonight, that would make it seven times. Seven times lucky.

Sarah sat up abruptly. Her lucky number was seven. What if the times lucky impostor's lucky number was seven too? Oh, no, thought Sarah. Her mouth was suddenly dry and she quickly sipped some tea. Immediately her head started buzzing and every part of her body felt weak. The tea, something's in the tea. I must get to Tom. That's where she's at. I have to end this tonight, whatever happens.

As she struggled to stand up, Sarah smelled the strong odor of gas. She stumbled to her feet. God, she was dizzy!! Weaving on trembling legs, she wobbled into the kitchen. The place reeked of gas. Sarah shut off the valves, but she was clumsy and slow and now choking on the fumes. Finally she flung the door open and stood there gasping as the smell cleared out. Her brain worked slower than usual, but she now realized she'd been meant to die here tonight. She must get to her children and Tom.

Her head had cleared some from the cool, night air, but still her mind was fuzzy enough to force her to drive slowly to the Pizza Palace.

"Mom, you decided to come anyway," Robbie jumped up and hugged Sarah. "Sit down by me," he said.

Tom smiled foolishly. "Gee, Sarah, you were so adamant about not coming. I'm glad you changed your mind."

Only Rachel said nothing. She stared intently at her mother for a full minute and then said, "Dad, I don't think I want to go to the movie."

"Wow, this is great pizza," Sarah was saying. I just love pepperoni."

Robbie swallowed a huge bite of pizza and then yelled, "Rachel, what's wrong with you? We've been waiting to see "The Lion King" forever. Why don't you want to go?"

Tom handed Sarah another slice of pizza. "Gee, Sarah, you have changed. You used to hate pepperoni."

"I guess I have," Sarah smiled. "Hurry and finish, Robbie. I can't wait to see the movie."

Tom chuckled, "Three pizzas. Don't tell me that's all you can eat?"

"Yeah, Dad, we're full. Let's go," said Robbie. Tom stood up and stretched. Well, if everyone's full, I'll go up and pay the bill. You all can relax here till I come back and then here we come Lion King."

"Rachel, you're so quiet tonight," Sarah said. "Don't you feel well?"

"No, Mom," Rachel stood up. "I'm just surprised you're here. You were so angry at Daddy and now your here eating pizza with him."

"That all happened in the past, Honey. I've forgiven Daddy and that's how it should be."

In the car Sarah finally spotted the Pizza Palace. Thank Goodness. What had been in that tea? She'd only taken a sip and she was still dizzy. Sarah gave up trying to park, and left the car sticking out halfway in the street. She was terrified. She had no idea what would happen when she confronted the duplicate, but she had no choice if she wanted to keep her family. She headed for the door.

In the restaurant, Robbie bounced out of his seat. "Let's wait for Dad by the door," he said. "I can't wait to see the movie."

"I really just want to go home," said Rachel. "I feel a little sick."

Sarah put her arm around Rachel as they walked toward the door. "Nonsense, Rachel," she said. "You'll feel better soon as you get a little fresh air."

Raising her arm, she signaled to Tom they'd be waiting outside and headed to the doorway.

As Sarah reached the doorway of the restaurant, she looked around. The street was quiet and dark, only a few cars passing. She hoped this wouldn't be her last look. She kept seeing those black demons in the movie dragging that man away, while his body lay in the street.

Suddenly in front of her the door opened. Out came Rachel, and right beside her the duplicate. Robbie was still in the restaurant.

"NO!!!" yelled the duplicate Sarah. "YOUR DEAD!!!! THIS IS MY FAMILY NOW!! WE CANNOT MEET!! WE CANNOT MEET!!!!"

But Sarah kept advancing, closer and closer. Suddenly she reached out and grabbed the impostor.

"NO NO NO NO!!!" she yelled as bolts of lightning flicked around her.

Rachel stood screaming. "Mom, oh Mom, I knew it wasn't you. I knew."

Robbie stood staring in shock through the open doorway.

The air around the two woman crackled louder and louder, but still Sarah held on. Bolts of light started at the impostor's feet and swirled around and around as it slowly enveloped her entire body. Sarah held on tightly as the woman in her hands turned into a huge ball of electricity. The only thing left of the impostor was her face and she was still yelling, "NOOOOOOOOOOO," and then she disappeared in a brilliant flash of blue light. Sarah swayed forward as Rachel grabbed her and through the door ran Tom and Robbie.

"What's going on here? What was that light?" yelled Tom as he picked up Sarah who was only half conscious in Rachel's arms. Along the street people were staring, not sure of what they'd just seen. Robbie was crying and Rachel trying to comfort him as they carried Sarah to the car.

Tom whispered, "It's all right, Sarah. I'm taking you to the hospital. You'll be O.K. as tears slipped down his cheeks.

Once they were in the car, Sarah sat up slowly. "Listen," she whispered weakly. "All of you. I'm all right. Just a little dizzy. She spiked my tea at home, but when I touched her, she just disintegrated. She's gone and I'm safe. Don't you see?" she said smiling. "I WON!!!"

"Sarah," Tom said quietly. "I don't pretend to know what happened back there, but I know you're my own sweet Sarah and I don't want to leave you alone tonight." Robbie and Rachel sitting in the back seat, stopped sniffling and came to full attention. "Yes, Tom, come home," whispered Sarah. "Come home and we can be a family again.

Later on that evening, when the children had finally gone to sleep, reassured by their parents that all was well, Sarah and Tom retired to their bedroom. They were eating microwaved pizza which was the only thing Tom could make and he wanted Sarah to rest. Now, Sarah, having finished her pizza, snuggled into bed and whispered, "Hurry up Tom. It's cold in here without you."

"Gee, Sarah," he said as he climbed into bed. "You ate the one with the pepperoni again. You used to hate it."

"I guess," Sarah said with a smile as she put her arms around Tom, "My tastes have changed."

The End

RING RING

The day dawned dark, dreary, and dismal. Bill woke slowly from the problems that followed him into sleep to the reality of another problem laden day. Sheets of rain slanted off his roof and pounded against the windows. Another cold March morning began.

"Oh no", he muttered, "Not more rain. Just what I need to lift my spirits." Next to his bed the phone jangled loudly. Ring ring ring ring.

"Hello", Bill answered.

"Mr. Johnson?" a clear crisp no-nonsense voice issued from the earpiece. This is Miss Nestor from Sears calling. You are three payments behind on your bill and we expect payment this Friday or this account will be turned over to a collection agency."

"But, but", Bill sputtered. "I explained all this to someone else from Sears. I've just been laid off. I've been trying to find a job. I'll send some money as soon as I get it."

"I'm afraid Mr. Johnson when you signed this contract with us, you agreed to pay this contract on time. When you can get it is just not good enough. Perhaps you should seek financial help."

"Bill yelled angrily into the phone, "How can I borrow money when I'm not working and can't repay it?"

"I'm afraid Mr. Johnson, that is your problem. We will expect payment by Friday." Then the phone clicked into silence.

"I've got to get some money", he thought, as he counted $51.26 in bills and change, the sole contents of his wallet. His checking account consisted of $100.00 and that plus his wallet was all the money he had in the world.

The old house Bill lived in was rented, although he had hopes of buying it one day. He never guessed the brilliant new job would downsize a year and a half after he started, and that good old Bill would be the first to go. Who would believe in this age of computers and cellular phones that jobs could be lost with such lightning speed?

Just a few months before the future seemed so much brighter. He had a few pieces of nice furniture and a job with a future. Then each day was an exciting new experience. Now he sold most of his furniture, and was down to one can of coffee, a half loaf of stale bread, and a box of cheerios, the total of his edible supplies. He faced each day in depression and feat. I must do something, he thought. Maybe there is something in the attic I can sell. Anything would be a help.

In the attic, even with the one dim light bulb lit, it was dark and dingy. Layers of dust covered everything. There wasn't much to see. An old couch sat in the corner ripped and dirty. No one would want that. A couple of kitchen chairs with taped plastic lay by the window. On the floor covered with dust lay a broken lawn chair and an old trunk. Bill thought. Maybe there's something in there I can use.

He grabbed an old towel off the floor and wiped off some of the dust. Then he pried the lid open with a rusty screwdriver he found nearby. Inside were piles of old blankets, a few old books, and stuck in the corner, a gleam of white plastic. Digging it out, he pulled from the dusty trunk a phone. It looked like a cordless phone. What would a cordless phone be doing with all this old stuff he wondered, and curiously it didn't look new. There was a huge scratch on the side. Maybe, he thought, I can pawn it. I should get something for it, at least enough to pay my Sear's bill. I'll have to try it first to make sure it works. He carried it downstairs, laid it by the basement sink to clean, and then went out into the wet, rainy day to begin another day of job hunting.

Bill arrived home tired and discouraged from his day of fruitless searching. It was no sir, we don't need any extra help right now, or we'll get back to you as soon as we have an opening, or just plain you are not qualified. What a day. Bill trudged up the steps to his bedroom, collapsed in his favorite chair, and tiredly pulled off his soaked shoes and socks. He made himself a cup of hot tea and wrapped himself up in his old fuzzy robe. Even though nothing had changed, he was just beginning to relax when the phone rang jarring him back to reality. Bill simply did not want to hear any more bad news today, so he only sat and stared at the phone until it stopped ringing on the fourteenth ring. It was then Bill remembered the old phone waiting to be cleaned in the basement with the answering machine. I'll hook that up, he thought. At least that can do my dirty work for a while and if it works right, I can still sell it, and maybe get a few bucks for it.

The next morning Bill woke up determined to make something positive happen that day. He called the electric company.

"G K L Electric", a bright cheery voice responded.

"Hi", Bill answered, I'm Bill Johnson at 1425 Hill Road and I am calling to reset up payment arrangements on my account."

"Could I please have your account number sir?" chirped the happy voice.

"Sure, it's 115 2891 680. I've been paying the current balance plus $10.00 but I missed payment last month because—"

"Just a minute sir, until I access your account."

Bill waited for about two minutes and then another voice came over the line not quite so cheery as the first.

"Sir", she said, "that total bill is now due because you defaulted on your payment."

Bill took a deep breath and answered. "That", Bill said very slowly, "is why I am calling. I lost my job three months ago and all my bills are behind until I can get another job."

"I'm sorry sir" the voice said briskly. "You were on a payment arrangement, and you defaulted. Now the entire bill is due."

"Didn't you hear me?" Bill yelled into the phone. "I just need a little more time."

"I'm sorry Mr. Johnson", the now cold voice answered. "The best I can do for you is to change your payment arrangements to $20.00 a month plus the bill and if these arrangements are not kept, we will be forced to disconnect your electricity, and I'm sure you are aware that there is a 75.00-dollar charge for reconnection and $100.00 security charge."

"That's right", Bill muttered. "Hit a man when he's down".

"Will that be satisfactory sir?", questioned the voice.

"But I can't", Bill answered, that will be fine, current bill plus $20.00 per month." "All right., all right, that will be fine, current bill plus $20.00 per month.

"Mr. Johnson, I will set up these new arrangements immediately. And remember we must have your payment by the 25th of the month or I will be unable to stop disconnection. Good afternoon, sir."

Bill made three more phone calls just like that and then gave up. No one was going to give him extra time or any kind of break. He spent the rest of the day cleaning and setting up his answering machine, straightening up the little house, and then finally fixing himself dinner.

At 5:30 the phone rang. On the third ring, the answering machine clicked on. *You've reached Bill Johnson. I can't get to the phone right now. Please leave a brief message after the beep and I'll call you right back.* Bill sat and listened to the telephone company telling him how delinquent he was. Then the little tape shut off. During the evening, Bill heard the phone ring three more times and the answering machine click on to answer. He felt a certain relief in not having to hear anymore ultimatums concerning his unpaid bills. At least his answering machine was working. He still hoped to sell it for good price. Just before Bill tiredly crawled into bed, he decided against his better judgment to play back his messages.

"You have three messages, sir". a soft, sexy voice whispered. *March 4th, 6:30 PM first message.*

Bill stared at the phone, as message one, two, and three rolled off the tape. The last message whirred to an end, and the husky soft, voice whispered *End of messages sir.*

That machine, thought Bill, has the voice of an angel. I wonder how it knew I was a sir. Bill smiled. Maybe I won't get rid of this phone so fast after all, he thought as he reached down and pressed the delete button.

All messages deleted sir.

Boy, Bill mused, I've just been threatened with disconnection from the gas, telephone, and cable company and I don't even care.

The next day, Thursday, Bill awakened early for he had an interview scheduled. Any job offers were few and far between these days, so he dressed carefully, anxious to make a good impression. As he drove downtown, he practiced answers to every conceivable question he could imagine. This job offer could well be his last chance for decent employment. His next move, he already knew would be the fast-food arena McDonald's or Burger King.

Bill arrived at Anderson's Department Store ten minutes before his interview and sat nervously down in the outer office. He had smooth down his salt and pepper hair and had adjusted his wire framed glass several times before a young attractive receptionist approached him and smiled. "Are you the 8:30?", she asked.

"Yes, that's me." Bill smiled. "I'm Bill Johnson and I'm here to see Mr. Terrell."

"Well Bill, Mr. Terrell would like you to fill out this application and then he'll see you."

Five minutes later the inner door opened, and she called, "Mr. Johnson, Mr. Terrell will see you now."

Oh boy, Bill thought, this is it, and then the door slammed shut behind him. John Terrell had acted as though the job was Bill's. Anderson's Store needed a new manager and Bill was well qualified. He seemed amply impressed by Bill's resumé and was delighted to learn Bill had attended the same college as him. I have two others to interview, were his parting words, but you can expect to hear from me within two weeks.

Horns beeped and traffic whizzed by as Bill drove down Main Street. It had gone great, and Bill knew he had the job. He just knew it. Oh, if only he had this job. But everything had gone exceptionally well. Hadn't it? "I really need this job" thought Bill, "and I'm going to get it. and I'm so sure my luck is changing that I'm going to celebrate with a meal in Simpson's." What better way to spend his last dollar?

With that, he pulled over into the parking lot of one of the best family restaurants in town.

From across the room Caroline wondered for the third time, could that be Bill Johnson? It certainly looked like him. Maybe a bit taller than she remembered and definitely more silver up on top, but just as handsome. Finally, when she saw he was sipping his end of meal coffee, she tentatively approached him.

"Bill, Bill Johnson, is that you?", she called. "I'm Caroline, remember Caroline Peterson from High School."

Bill glanced up surprised "Sure I remember you. You're Carrie, Carrie Peterson. Boy, have you changed? Sit down and have desert with me. You're certainly looking well, Carrie. How have you been all these years?"

"As opposed to being fat Carrie Peterson. Is that what you meant Bill?" "I remember Bill, Carrie, Carrie, big as a ferry, but I do have to admit you were one of the few who didn't join in."

Bill swallowed so fast he choked on his cake. "I'm sort of ashamed of that. I didn't do much to stop it either," he answered. "But you certainly look like you have put that behind you now."

Caroline smoothed a stray wrinkle from her navy-blue suit. Sleek and short, it clung in all the right places. "Yes, I'm back in town for good. I finally passed the bar. You are now looking at a full pledged lawyer at Jacobson, Jacobson, Peterson, and Sloan."

"Well, in that case," Bill smiled, "I hope to see a lot more of you. But now that you're a successful lawyer, you might not want to waste time with me. I've just come from my last chance interview. About three months ago, I lost my job without a dime to back me up. You are dining today with one of the recently unemployed.

Caroline leaned forward, her long, dark brown hair brushing her cheek as she slipped a tiny white card into Bill's hand. "This is my home phone", she said. "Call me, and if you're the Bill I used to know, this situation is only temporary. My bets are on you, Bill."

With that Caroline stood and exited the restaurant, while every man present sat riveted to her long slender legs in navy blue pumps. Bill drove home elated. A good prospect for a job and a beautiful woman interested in him all in one day. His luck must be changing.

A few weeks later, Bill awoke with a start. Of course, today was the twenty-fifth, disconnection day for the electric. Oh no, Bill thought, I can't let them do that now, not when things are just beginning to improve. Bill grabbed the phone and began frantically dialing the electric company.

"G K L Electric, Veronica speaking."

"Yes, Bill responded, "I need to speak to whoever stops disconnections."

"Sir, just a minute. Could you at least give me your account number?"

"All right, all right, it's 115 2891 680 but I need to talk to the manager or someone. I cannot have my electric disconnected today."

"Sir, are you sure that is the correct account number?"

"Of course," Bill answered, "Why are you asking?"

"Because, sir, that account, Bill Johnson at 1425 Hill Road has a balance of zero"

"What do you mean?", Bill asked. "You mean I'm already an inactive account."

"NO sir, No sir. It means your mistaken. You are not scheduled for cut off. Our records are showing you owe nothing on this account. This account is paid in full. Good morning, sir."

"But, but", Bill sputtered and then realized he was listening to a dial tone. Bill stood staring at the dead phone in his hand. Zero balance. That was impossible. There was no way that bill was paid. What could be happening? Of course, it must be an error. One of their computers had slipped a disc or confused his account with someone else's. At least it gave him a little extra time.

"This is my lucky day!", yelled Bill.

The sun had just completed its journey across Bill's bedroom floor as he very carefully replaced the receiver. He stared blankly at the spring like March Day outside his window. Every company that had left him threatening messages was paid in full. He couldn't believe it. Zero balances on all his bills. Almost as though, Bill stopped pacing and stared at the phone. Almost as though they had been deleted. No, no, that was impossible. But it was also impossible that six companies could make such serious mistakes. It couldn't be but what if, what if there was something unexplainable going on with the phone. As Bill stood contemplating it, it jangled loudly. Bill grabbed the phone on the second ring. "Hello."

"Bill, Bill is that you? This is Caroline calling. I want to invite you to a wedding.

"A wedding?", Bill asked, "Whose getting married?'

"Yes, my best friend Marie is tying the knot, and I need an escort, and you were my first choice. Would you go with me?"

"Sure", Bill replied, "I'd love to. What do I need to do?"

"Nothing", answered Caroline. "Just be your own sweet self and wear a suit. I'll pick you up Saturday morning ten o' clock, and oh, Bill."

"Yes", answered Bill.

"Who is that woman who answers your phone? I thought you said you live alone?"

"I do", replied Bill.

"That must have been my answering machine."

"Answering Machine. No, this didn't sound like a machine. English accent, perfect diction, soft cultured voice. She told me Mr. Johnson was otherwise engaged and would be unavailable indefinitely, when I called you earlier."

"But that's not my message," declared Bill.

"Well you better check out that answering machine. Pick you up on Saturday. Bye."

Saturday morning arrived crisp and clear, and Bill was in exceptional spirits. Yesterday, Mr. Terrell's secretary had called and left a message. He was to report to Personnel 9:00 AM Monday morning. Bill was sure the job was his and just to be extra sure, he committed the message to memory on his answering machine. Naturally, he didn't think there was anything strange going on with the phone, but just to be on the safe side. Now Bill and Caroline were on their way to the wedding, and he felt more relaxed and happy than he felt in a long time.

The wedding was lovely. Caroline sat next to Bill in a softly ruffled, low necked, dusty blue dress. With her hair swinging freely, she looked younger and more vulnerable than Bill had ever seen her. Gone was the sleek, sophisticated image she usually cultivated. Together they watched the couple kneeling at the altar, as they repeated the prayers and took the final vows that united them as man and wife. As the soft tones of the singer began the final wedding hymn, Bill reached over and clasped Caroline's hand gently in his. She glanced up and smiled when she saw the unshed tears in his eyes mirroring her own.

Later on at the reception, Bill found himself attracted to this new gently Caroline more and more. They danced all the slow dances together, barely swaying in time to the music. At midnight, when almost everyone had left, Caroline and Bill congratulated Marie and her new husband Gary and kissed them both good-byes. As Caroline and Bill exited the side door, Marie called out, "from the way things looked tonight Carrie, yours may be the next wedding", and then she and her new husband drove off to enjoy their honeymoon.

On the way home Bill drove, and Caroline snuggled against him all the way. When they reached Caroline's house, she invited Bill in. Bill readily accepted, and the next morning found Bill thoroughly entrenched in Caroline's bed and Caroline entrenched in Bill's heart.

Several months later, on a warm romantic, starlit evening in June, Bill asked Caroline to marry him. He was now a full-fledged manager at Anderson's and doing well. He had no debts, and had refurnished his little house. He even had a small bank account. Things were great and he loved Carrie. Why wait any longer?

"Oh yes, Bill, you knew that would be my answer", "What took you so long?" she laughed.

"Oh Carrie, I'm so glad you picked that particular day to eat in Simpson's. It was a lucky day for me. You must know how much I love you," he whispered.

Bill bent forward and kissed her tenderly. Then he reached for her hand, and slipped a shining diamond ring on her finger. When Bill climbed tiredly into bed that night, he gave a sigh of happiness. All of his problems had disappeared and now he was going to marry a wonderful woman. He looked at the scratched plastic phone next to his bed.

"You can bet I'll never sell you. You're my good luck charm", he whispered as he fell asleep.

The next week Carrie called Bill to finalize the plans for their wedding. On the third ring the answering machine clicked on. *You've reached Bill Johnson. I'm not home right now. Please leave a brief message and I'll call you right back.*

"Bill, It's Carrie, I just want to let you know. The rehearsal is tonight and"

And you will never marry.

Carrie gasped, "Who is this?"

Me, why I'm Bill's answering machine and I will take no messages you.

Then Carrie heard the whir of the tape and a loud click. That evening Carrie drove to Bill's house to pick him up.

"Carrie, why didn't you call?", he asked.

"I did", she whispered while standing in the doorway. "You must get rid of that telephone. There's something really weird about it. It talked back to me today."

"OK Carr, the joke is over. I'll get ready."

"But Bill, I'm not joking. It talked to me today."

"Carr, it's supposed to talk to you. It's an answering machine. I know you think it's a piece of junk, Carrie but I regard it as my good luck charm. I can't get rid of it just because you don't like it."

"But Bill, All right", she whispered. "You call me because it won't let me call you." Bill just chuckled as they drove away. Several days later, one of Bill's friends called.

After Bill's message played, the friend Pete said "HI Bill. Got your invitation to the wedding. I just need instructions on getting to the church. When you get back"—

Hello sir, cut in a woman's voice. This is Bill's secretary. I'm telling anyone who calls that the wedding has been postponed indefinitely.

"Yeah, I hear ya, but why?', asked Pete.

Let's just say there has been some disagreement with the two parties involved. Good night, sir.

The next day the minister called confirming the church reservation. After Bill's message played Pastor Brown said, "Oh Bill, sorry I missed you. Just confirming Sunday, July 22nd, as date of your wedding. Let me know by tonight so I can have the bulletins printed."

Hello, Pastor Brown, a soft accented voice responded. I'm Bills answering service. He has informed me that his wedding is canceled.

"But I'm the minister. Why is it I have heard nothing about this?" asked Pastor Brown.

Why he didn't explain his decision to me but I will definitely give him your message.

Pastor Brown hung his phone up and sat down carefully. "I just don't believe this" he thought. "Either Caroline or Bill would have called me. And they seem so in love. I'm going to call Caroline." Three times Pastor Browhn called Caroline's house and the line was busy. Finally he dialed again and this time the phone rang. Caroline answered on the second ring.

"Oh Pastor Brown, I'm glad you called. Bill and I are all set for Sunday. Are the bulletins printed?"

"But, but", the pastor sputtered. "Some answering service at Bill's house just told me the wedding was canceled."

Cold chills traveled down Carrie's back as she stood there clutching the phone.

"Carrie, are you there?" called the pastor.

"Yes, I'm still here," she whispered. "Look Pastor Brown, the wedding is definitely on. The woman you talked to is some jealous employee of Bill's. I'll let him know about this so he can be forewarned. But you can bet we will both be there bright and early July twenty-second."

"Well, I'm certainly relieved to hear everything's all right. I had a hard time reaching you tonight. Your phone was busy so long. But I'm glad to know that my two favorite people are going to be at this wonderful wedding.

But as Carrie slowly hung up the phone, she wondered if anybody else would. That evil machine! How many others had it told the wedding was off? And she hadn't been on the phone all night. How could her line be busy? I can't tell Bill, she thought. He has a mental block concerning that machine, so I have to somehow keep him away from that house until after we're married. Five minutes later, Carrie was on her way to Bill's office to pick him up from work. She intercepted him just as he was getting in his car.

"Bill" she yelled. "The minister called. Everything's all set for the wedding but for the next two nights, you're going to stay with the best man and the bridesmaids are staying at my house. Everyone will be together, and it will be easier on Sunday."

Bill seemed a little confused, but he agreed to the change and they picked up his tux on the way home. So two days later, the grand wedding went off as planned, and if there were several empty spots in the church, the out of town people, Bill never seemed the wiser.

After their wedding, they left immediately for their honeymoon and were so busy when they returned, packing and moving their belongings together that Carrie forgot all about the incident until she saw the dreaded object all set up in Bill's office. By then she was so happy with Bill she didn't want to spoil it, so she said nothing about it.

Traffic horns honked loudly combining with the screech of brakes as Bill drove eagerly down Main Street. He was trying his best to stay within the speed limit, but he could not wait to get out of city traffic and on to Green Meadow Road which led to his new house in the country. Today he'd just been put in charge of three new Anderson stores across the country. He couldn't wait to tell Carrie, his wife of three years. She would be so proud. She had given up her own law practice one year ago, when they moved to their new split-level in the country. It was a beautiful house bordered on one side by a small brook, and on the other by the woods. Directly behind the house Carrie planted a huge garden she loved to work in. Often she would spot a deer, nibbling on her vegetables planted near the fence. Bill would stand by the kitchen window enjoying the sight of his beautiful wife in her shorts and halter, pulling weeds in the garden. Of course, now that she was three months pregnant, she might not be wearing that halter much longer. Bill decided to stop at a roadside stand on the way home where they sold fantastic roses. Just the thing to get their celebration off to a good start.

Caroline got home early from her doctor's appointment. Today she was told the sex of the baby and she couldn't wait to tell Bill. She lay two large steaks on the counter to cook for the celebration meal. She set the table with her best china and silver, then to complete the effect, she decided to get a bottle from the wine cellar. She dreaded going down there because it was poorly lighted and the wine cellar was another flight down under the house. But she wanted everything perfect when Bill arrived, so down she went to get the wine.

Caroline just selected the bottle she wanted when the cellar door slammed shut. Oh no, in her haste, she forgot to prop the door open and now she was locked in. The door had a latch that automatically locked when the door closed, and now she was stuck down here unless, unless. Thank God. She still had her cell phone in her coat pocket, which she'd never taken off. She dialed Bill's car phone number. The phone clicked and buzzed and then a familiar woman's voice came on the line.

Hello Carrie, the voice said. *I've been waiting for you to do something stupid. I'm deeply afraid you won't get to talk to Bill today. But I'll give him a message for you. You just make yourself comfortable because I'm afraid you will be down there for a long time.*

Then Caroline sat helplessly in the cellar listening to the phone complete her call. The line connected to Bill's car phone and Caroline could hear Bill answer.

"Hello."

Mr. Johnson, the voice said, *I'm afraid I have some bad news concerning your wife.*

"What?" yelled Bill. "Who is this? What's wrong with Carrie?"

Well, I'm Nurse Andrews at the hospital. Caroline was in today. She was having abdominal pain and I'm sorry to tell you she lost the baby.

"Oh no!!" Bill yelled. "But she was fine this morning. Where is she?"

That's why I'm calling, Mr. Johnson. She was so upset that we sent her to a hospital in New York that not only has an excellent medical staff, but they also specialize in severe depression.

"Where?" whispered Bill. Please tell me where?"

It's called Jonas State Hospital and the address is 2528 West Central. I'm sorry to give you such sad news but I'm sure she'll be all right.

Bill slammed down the phone and turned back to the highway. The only thing he could think of was to get to his Carrie.

At the moment, his Carrie was screaming into the phone. "No Bill. No, it's not true. I'm right here at home. Please Bill, please hear me."

Now she slowly hung up the phone. That horrible machine finally did it. She was stuck here in the cellar, and Bill sent on a wild goose trip to Lord knows where. She sat down on one of the old wooden wine crates to think. Then jumping up again she frantically searched through the shelves of wine but there was nothing there to eat and only wine to drink. She slumped back on her crate and began to cry. Bitter, angry tears. Today was to be a celebration. She stared angrily at the door. God, she'd give anything to get her hands on that horrible piece of plastic. For years she'd been terrified of it. Now all she felt was a blinding rage it had ruined this special night.

It was damp in the cellar and Caroline searched the whole area again until she found an old moth-eaten blanket stuffed under the paint shelf. She finally found an area that looked reasonably clear of debris. Then she used her coat for a pillow and wrapped the old blanket around her. As she fluffed her coat, a forgotten pack of saltines fell out, and Caroline eagerly opened them and munched. She had been down here for hours and now fear crept back. If that thing meant to harm her, it would do it before Bill returned. Now thoroughly frightened, she lay shaking and worrying until shear exhaustion forced her to sleep. Then the world of her nightmares took over.

Caroline awoke suddenly. In the one small space where Caroline could see out, dawn was breaking. Calmer now, Caroline took stock of her options. If Bill drove all the way to New York trying to find her, it would take him three days to get there and back. He would probably drive back thinking there was no emergency and that someone made a mistake. If he called, that hated machine would convince him everything was fine. She was stuck down here days without food or water and that plastic monster was betting she wouldn't make it.

All day Caroline tried to pry open the locked door with whatever she could find in her jail. Finally tired, thirsty, and hungry she sat down on her makeshift bed and sipped some of the wine. She knew she shouldn't because of the baby, but it seemed the lesser evil. The wine made her sleepy and just as her tired body succumbed, she heard the phone ring.

The next morning, she was noticeably weaker and she knew she had to get out somehow. Bill had called. She dimly remembered hearing the phone ring just as she slipped off to sleep. So, no help there. Someone from outside would help her but how. Then she remembered. The car, her car. They were coming to check the brakes. When they came, she would somehow get their attention. Tiredly, she piled wine crates under the window. Finally, she had enough boxes in place to get her face to the window. She wedged herself in place to wait. She patted her rounded belly gently and whispered, "Don't worry, little lady. We'll get out of this."

An hour later, her legs were numb when she saw a truck pull into the driveway. Al's Garage was printed on the side.

"Help", she screamed as soon as they got out of the truck. "Help, I'm locked down here. Help."

One of the men walked over and peered in the window. "Hey, Al", he yelled. "There's a lady locked in there."

"Please get me out", called Caroline.

"Just hang on, lady. We'll get you out", called one of the men as he tried to open the cellar window. The other man went to try the back door.

Finally, after what seemed like hours, Caroline heard the cellar door opening. She stumbled off the boxes and right into the arms of Al himself.

"Take it easy, lady." He said while helping her up the steps. "You're O.K. now."

Caroline wept with relief while the other man said, "Look, lady. Do you think we should take you to the hospital? Let them check you out."

Caroline collapsed weakly in the big easy chair as one the men went to get her something to eat. "No, no, I'm all right", she whispered. "Just tired and hungry."

Eagerly she ate soup as the two men looked on. As she sat resting, she heard the familiar rumble of the garbage truck coming down the street. The men were shouting back and forth as they tossed garbage into the huge rolling conveyor.

Suddenly, Caroline jumped up. Exhausted as she was, new strength flowed into her body as she raced up the steps. Into Bill's office she ran. She snatched up the phone in a fury, wires flew everywhere, and then she raced back down and outside. She reached the curb just as the truck rolled up and in the huge conveyor, she tossed the phone. With great satisfaction, she watched it disappear and be crushed with all the other garbage.

"Thank God", she whispered. "It's gone forever". Then one of the mechanics caught her as tiredly stumbled back to the house. Hours later after she finished her sandwich and soup, and was tucked comfortably on the couch, the two mechanics decided she seemed well enough to leave.

"Now you call 911 if you feel sick or anything", called Al. "We don't like leaving you here alone, but if you're sure you'll be all right."

"I'm fine, she whispered already dozing off. "I'm safe now", she mumbled. "That horrid thing is gone".

"O.K. Mrs. Johnson. We'll take the car and be on our way. You take it easy now."

The next day around three o'clock Bill returned. They met at the door. Locked in each other's arms they hugged and hugged.

Finally Bill said, "The baby's really all right?"

"Oh yes, Bill, that phone of yours almost killed us but it's gone forever now." Bill stared at her in shock as she related the events of the past two days.

"Oh my God, Carrie. That's unbelievable! Thank God you're all right. But I called and talked to you. You explained everything. That's why I wasn't worried."

Carrie shook her head sadly. "Not me, you didn't talk to me, Bill".

"Oh Lord, you tried to tell me and I never believed you. Thank goodness for those mechanics."

"Yes, Bill, but it's gone forever. Your lucky piece".

"Lucky piece! Carrie, it almost took away the two things I love most in this world. It's no lucky piece to me."

Later that evening Bill told his good news and Carrie told his baby daughter. It was a magical night and they vowed never that phone again.

Several days later, Bill received a weird phone call.

"I would like to speak to Caroline Peterson, please", an angry feminine voice asked.

"You must mean Carrie Johnson, my wife", Bill answered.

"I don't care what her name is now. She's the one who put my husband in jail", the voice responded.

"Who is this?' Bill asked angrily.

"I'm Amy Sanders. Remember Samuel Sanders 8-10".

"But he was found guilty," Bill replied. "There was an eyewitness at that jewelry store."

"She was mistaken. It was someone else that looked like Sam and now I've come into some money, and I'm going to reopen the case, so you better warn your wife."

"Oh no", Bill answered. "My wife is pregnant, and she doesn't need this stress now. Besides your husband practically admitted his guilt of robbing that jewelry store."

"No, he didn't", and I'm going to prove it." Then she hung up.

When Carrie arrived home from grocery shopping, she noticed Bill seemed upset, but when she questioned him, he denied anything was wrong.

The next day just as he was leaving work, Dan Morrison, one of Bill's employees yelled. "Hey, Mr. Johnson. I just heard the Anderson Stores are downsizing. Do you think I'll lose my job?"

"Well Dan," Bill answered. I don't have any information on that but I'll look into for you and let you know."

"You know I heard they were going to get rid of the management first anyway", called Dan.

Bill continued to his car but when he reached it, his hands were shaking so he could hardly unlock the car door.

"Nonsense", he whispered, as he drove home. "It couldn't happen again".

That night after dinner, Bill and Carrie were drinking coffee in the living room. A summer breeze was moving the sheer, white curtains. Bill gazed at his tastefully furnished living room surrounded by soft beige walls. He could see directly through the windows to his well-manicured lawn outside. Sitting in the driveway sat two Mercedes side by side. A blue one for him and red one for Carrie. He gave a huge sigh.

"What's wrong, Honey?" Carrie asked hesitantly. "You seem so sad and preoccupied tonight."

Bill shook his head as if to clear it. The he hugged Carrie and rubbed his hand across her expanding belly.

"Nothing is wrong", he said fiercely. "Everything is perfect and always will be."

Two blocks down the street at the city dump, two men Jose' and Big Mike were emptying the compacted garbage. "Hey Mike," called Jose', "look at this".

"What is it Jose'?" answered Mike.

"Look at this phone. It went through the crusher but there's nothing on it but one scratch."

"So, what?", Mike yelled back, "It probably doesn't work. You saw how anxious that lady was to get rid of it."

"But maybe it does work", called Jose'. "I'm going to take it home and try it out. If it works, I'll have me an answering machine.

"You sure will." Mike laughed, clapping Jose' on the back. "I say go for it!!"

VANISHED

VANISHED

"Mom, the fair is coming. The fair is coming. Look, half the rides are up already," little Jake shouted to his Mom.

She smiled fondly at him.

"Yes, we'll have lots of fun there, Honey, but at least give them time to get it built. We'll go there tomorrow when they're all finished."

"O.K. Mom," said Jake. "I'm going to sit here and watch them build it while I drink my coke."

"Sure, Honey, but it will be lunch time soon."

Jake Johnson and his mother Sara lived just across the street from the huge park that sponsored the fair every year, so they had a ringside seat for all the festivities. They experienced the concerts, the stock car races, the animal shows, the scary rides and the fantastic smells as they cooked sausage sandwiches, funnel cakes, hot dogs, etc.

Jake sat on the porch all afternoon and watched as the rides went up almost magically. He just couldn't wait. He didn't even want to leave to eat his lunch, but his mother made him come in.

"Come now Jake," she said sternly. It's not as if you've never been there before."

"I can't help it, Mom. It's just so much fun."

"Well, Jakie boy, I have a lot of free passes so I'm sure you'll get your fill of it."

The next day at 6:00 PM on the dot, Jake and his mother went to the fair. They ate funnel cakes and laughed at their powder sugar

140

beards. they munched french fries and hot dogs and they rode all the rides. The ferris wheel which held them breathlessly up in the air, the Himalayas which spun backwards and forwards blasting out the latest pop music. They stayed till the fair closed.

Jake was so tired he was falling asleep as they walked home, but still as he was tucked into bed, he murmured tiredly, "we're going tomorrow, aren't we Mom?"

His Mom bent, kissed his forehead, and whispered, "you bet we are. Now you go to sleep."

Before his Mom was out of the room, he was sound asleep.

The next night it rained. How it rained. Great crashes of thunder and flashes of lightening, and no matter how Jake pleaded, Sara refused to go to the fair.

"We have two more days to go, Honey and it's not like you haven't seen everything there already."

So, Jake had to content himself with sitting on the front porch and watching the scads of people run home from the fair. The concert, however continued, the throbbing drums blending in with the crashes of thunder.

Sara, sitting at the kitchen table with a cup of coffee and her newspaper, wondered how anyone could be brave enough to sit through a concert like that. The newspaper proclaimed the fair to be a huge success. The concerts were fabulous, the games were bringing in scads of money and even the freak shows were doing well, but way down at the bottom of the page in a small section barely seen was another article.

Three small boys disappear at fair, it read. It went on to say that their parents dropped them off at Gate 2 and watched them enter the fair. When the parents returned at 10:00 to take them home at the same gate, the boys weren't there. The worried parents searched the whole fair twice but found no sign of them. Finally, they engaged several police officers to help, but though they searched until the fair closed, the boys were not found. The police seemed to think the boys had just wandered away, but the parents knew that was not the case.

Sara stopped reading. God, she thought. Suppose there was some lunatic who was snatching children at the fair. She was glad it would be gone in two days, and from now on Jake was holding his hand while they were there or else they weren't going. Now she called him off the porch not wanting him out of her sight a moment longer.

The next night Jake was surprised at how his Mom clung to him not letting go of his hand at all.

"Mom," he said over and over. "I'm not a baby."

But still she held on to him tightly.

"There's a lot of strange people at these fairs," she answered. "You stay close to me."

Jake noticed she didn't seem to be having much fun either. Then Jake smiled. He knew what should make her laugh.

"Look, Mom," he said. "The freak show. Let's go see the freak show. That'll cheer you up."

Sure enough, right in front of them, a battered old sign professed, COME SEE THE SEVEN WONDERS OF THE WORLD!!!

"Only $1.00. Come in and see marvels that you've never seen before," an old man with a battered gray hat and salt and pepper hair and a long grizzly beard stood at the tent opening yelling.

"Now, Jakey," Sara said. "You know those are all fakes. There are no real freaks in there. For $1.00," and she laughed her musical laugh.

Jake, just glad he'd made her smile said, "I know, Mom. At least well have a good laugh."

The old man standing at the tent opening fixed both of them with a ferocious scowl, but he eagerly accepted their dollar bills as they went inside. Sure enough, most of the freaks were wax figures posed to look frightening. The only thing that looked real was a two headed baby soaking in a corroded jar of some slimy looking liquid. Jake just felt repulsed by this. What mother was so poor, she given her baby to this disgusting old man to exhibit her sorrows forever. As they reached the end of the tent, Jake said, "you were right, Mom. They're all fakes. Let's go."

Sara smiled. "Yes," she said. "Let's get out of this smelly place."

The old man still watching them angrily from the shadows whispered. "You won't say that next time lady. You and that little animal will never trash my show again." Then he smiled cruelly. "Animal, yes that's exactly it."

That evening, Sara watched the fair from her porch glad that it was leaving tomorrow. She didn't know why she had such a sense of foreboding, but she knew she wanted that fair to leave town.

Upstairs in his bedroom, Jake watched from his window. One more day and the fair would be gone. He didn't know why his mother suddenly disliked the fair but he still loved it. Just one more day to enjoy it. As he watched, the rides stopped whirling one by one and the lights flickered out. Twelve o'clock. The fair was over for tonight. Crowds of people were pouring out the exits and in minutes, the fairgrounds were dark and silent.

Jake was about to snuggle under the blankets when he saw what looked like a light in the middle of the fairgrounds. He sat up eagerly. What could that light be? It seemed brighter. Now very faintly he could hear music coming from that area. Maybe they were having a special show at night.

Jake jumped out of bed, put on his shoes, and tiptoed to his Mom's room. She lay sound asleep, her glasses still on and the television still blaring away.

Jake smiled. He turned off the TV and put her glasses on the night stand. He was just going to sneak up to the fair to see what that light was. Mom would never know. He'd be back in two minutes. He was just going to put his coat on, run up and peek, and then go back to bed.

So one minute later Jake was walking through the gate into the darkened fairgrounds. He shivered as the hulking shapes of the rides appeared to be huge monsters in the dark, but as he moved closer to the light he felt braver. Now he could see it was the tent of the freak shows. He really didn't want to go in there again, but even as he hesitated, he saw two other little boys go in. Maybe he could just peek in the doorway. Something about the music seemed to bring him closer to the little tent.

"Come right in little man," said a creepy voice as a huge hairy hand closed over his arm. "Come right in and join us. One more little boy to add to my collection."

The next morning Sara woke early. She was in a fantastic mood. She fixed Jake's breakfast and called cheerfully, "come on Jakey. Breakfast is ready!!" No answer. Sara brightly called again. Still no answer.

"Jakey, what are you doing?", Sara called as she ran up the steps and approached his room. Jake's room was empty and the bathroom was empty Sara checked out the entire house but Jake wasn't to be found.

"Oh, No," she screamed. That damn fair. I knew something would happen. Hysterically she dialed the police department.

"Riverton Police Department," a deep masculine voice answered.

"I need your help. My little boy has disappeared," yelled Sara.

"Whoa, Lady, calm down. How do you know he's not playing with his friends? How old is he?"

"Look!," shouted Sara. He's only seven. He was in his pajamas and slippers. He wouldn't go anywhere like that. Someone has kidnapped him."

All right, Lady calm down. We'll send someone over to your house. Just give me your address."

After giving out the information needed, Sara stood, with tears in her eyes staring at the fair. The last day and she knew that Jake's disappearance had something to do with that fair. When the police arrived, after answering the usual routine questions, Sara convinced them to search the fair.

"We went up there everyday. If someone wanted to get him to go with them, they'd just have to mention fair. Hurry," Sara sobbed, "we have to search every exhibit. The fair leaves today."

"All right," Tom the big burley officer said. "Let's check out the fair."

The two officers and Sara checked every tent and exhibit. The officers were allowed to walk through each tent and search each exhibit, but there was no sign of Jake.

Finally, officer Tom said, "Mrs. Jackson, we've checked everywhere. Your boy is not here." Sara surveyed the whole fair. There was something different.

"The freak show," she shouted. The freak show is gone. It was right there last night. We, joked, Jake and I, about how sorry it was. I bet he stole my son. The other officer called Mac said, "Well we can ask the fair officers and try to find out where he went but other than that, all we can do is put Jake's picture all around town and hope someone recognizes him."

When they reached the main office, a Mr. Dunkin got up from his desk to shake hands with Tom.

"The Freak Show? oh yeah, he packed up his tent and left last night. Said he'd meet us at the next stop. He wasn't making any money. Said he was going to round up some freaks and join us in Florida.

"Is that usual?" asked Tom. "Your acts just leave the fair anytime they choose?"

"No. Mr. Dunkin replied. "That's not our usual policy but he was all riled up about what some customer said about his show, and he was right. I don't believe his tent brought in a $100.00 all week. So, we told him, all right but if he didn't do better on our next gig, we'd have to get rid of him. So, he took off in a huff."

Sara felt like screaming. Her son was gone and there seemed like there was nothing she could do about it. She knew that decrepit old man had something to do with it but no one knew where he was, and he wouldn't be in Florida for four months. After pleading with the Police Department to check him out the minute he arrived in Florida, there was little else she could do. She went home to grieve in private.

The two officers walked Sara home and then stood sheepishly twisting their hats not knowing how to ease the grief.

"We'll find him. Don't you worry, Miss. If he can be found, we'll find him." Then they climbed hurriedly into their police car and drove away leaving Sara standing in the doorway. Day after lonely day dragged by, everyone a day of sorrow for Sara. To compound her sorrow she saw Jake's picture everywhere, on milk cartons, telephone poles, even in the post office. At night she dreamed about finding Jake and just as she grabbed his hand, she'd wake to find Jake still gone and another torturing day to live through.

Time passed with Sara just existing through each day. Eventually her friends stopped trying to cheer her up and finally stopped talking to her as she never acknowledged them or replied back. One day when she arrived home from work something shook her out of herself imposed trance.

There were fair signs all over. That dreaded fair was coming again. Well I'm not going anywhere near it, Sara thought. I should've moved somewhere else long ago.

Sara closed all her windows to seal out the music and noises of the fair. The house was like an oven in the hot August heat, but she suffered in the stifling house trying to escape the gayety of the fair. Near the end of the week a strange thought occurred to Sara. If Jake had disappeared with the fair, maybe he was still there. Of course, Jake would come back home if he could, but maybe he'd lost his memory. Sara decided to go to the fair just to check out every exhibit just in case. Tomorrow the fair was leaving again, so her last chance was tonight.

Reluctantly she left the house to go to the fair. Without Jake, entering those fairgrounds was torture. She moved from booth to booth like a robot wishing she hadn't come. Suddenly she spotted the freak show, but what a change, no little painted sign now but a marquee, letters sparkling in bright red.

COME ONE

COME ALL

SEE THE SEVEN WONDERS OF THE WORLD

ONLY $10.00

Sara gasped. $10.00 for those stick figures she'd seen last year. But, no, something was different. This tent was huge and a young attractive girl was taking the money Sara had to see this.

Inside huge cages were set at eye level so one could see each exhibit clearly. The first thing she saw looked like a huge cat until she saw its face. The face, there was no other way to describe it looked human. She had big, beautiful blue eyes and eyelashes, a tiny little nose, but under that were whiskers and a cat's mouth. She made little mewling noises and her eyes moved over the crowd ceaselessly, but it was her expression that astonished Sara. It was pure misery.

The next exhibit was a small squirrel like animal. It resembled a squirrel in every way except for the claws. It had tiny hands like a little girl and the eyes were a lovely shade of green. Sara gasped. These creatures really were freaks. Sara shuddered. I don't want to see any more of this, she thought hurrying to the exit. She was almost to the tent flap when she heard the most pathetic cry of all.

"MAHHHHHHHH" it called in hoarse sounding doggy voice. "MAHHHHHHHHH"

Sara turned and there sat a tiny dog. It lay at the front of the cage, it's claws wrapped around the bars.

"MAHHHHHHHHHHH" it moaned again and Sara saw the face. It was Jake's face. Her son's face on a dog and it was crying, tears rolling down its little furry face. Sara grasped at its face and burst into tears as it pressed closer to her hand. It was Jake! Oh My God, she thought. NO, No, her mind screamed and then the old man was at her side smiing gleefully into her agonized face.

"How do you like my fakes now?" he whispered just as Sara fainted.

TEN WISHES

Joe Parker was starting fifth grade today. He was going to a new school, and he was beyond excited. Everything had to go right today. It just had to. But the fates seemed to be against him. While he was brushing his teeth and making faces in the mirror, the sink backed up and overflowed. He had to call Mom who had to clear up the mess and they were all late getting to the car. Not a good start.

When they reached the school, Joe's Mom parked across the street to see him safely across. As usual the crossing guard was nowhere in sight. Joe stood on the sidewalk waiting patiently for the traffic to at least slow down. Behind his Mom's cars someone else pulled up and let out their little girl who immediately ran across the street. Then he proceeded to beep his horn loudly at Joe's Mom.

"Stupid man", she yelled. "Go around me. I'm waiting for my son to cross the street."

Then she motioned angrily for him to go.

Joe jumped. Was Mom yelling at him like that? Maybe. He flew across the street directly in front of a car. After a violent blast of horn and the swish of air as the car almost brushed the back of his legs. He made it to the other side. He glanced towards his mother, but she was already driving off. He walked slowly into the school. What a way to start the day he thought.

Joe found his homeroom without any trouble. Thank God, he thought gratefully as he sank into a seat. Several of his friends sat near him and soon Joe was chatting away and feeling much better.

"The subject of the day is Egyptian artifacts", said Mr. Flag, their teacher. "I'm sure you're going to find them very interesting. I have an exhibit in the art room which we are all going to tour. You are allowed to look, but not touch, understand? Some of these things are very fragile."

The class filed quietly into the art room, and they were astounded. On every table sat glorious golden deities that were worshipped by ancient Egyptians. There were lion headed sekhmets, cat headed bastets, and falcon headed horus, all made of gold and gleaming brightly on the cloth covered tables. The children walked through looking at the statues in wonder. Joe Was entranced by a tiny gold pen with Isis on the top and something which he couldn't quite read on the bottom. When he looked up, the teacher was leading the class out of the room. Joe was the last one. Just as he passed the table to leave, he grasped the golden pen and quickly slipped it in his pocket. Then they were walking back to their classroom. Joe's heart beat a frantic tattoo against his chest as they sat back down in their seats. What had he done? The pen had tantalized him. Now it lay burning a hole in his pocket.

Mr. Flag went on teaching the class unaware anything had happened. When the class ended, everyone filed out the door to the next class. As Joe passed, Mr. Flag grabbed Joe's shoulder. Oh no, thought Joe this is it.

"The next time you're in my class, Joe you'll pay attention to me not draw pictures on your notebook all hour, understand?" said Mr. Flag squeezing Joe's shoulder painfully.

"O.K, O.K.", yelled Joe. "I get it." Under his breath he whispered, "Thank God he doesn't know about the artifact, the old pig nose."

A flash of light sizzled through the classroom and when Joe looked up, Mr. Flag's nose was flat with two huge holes just like a pig. The few kids that were left were giggling wildly and pointing. Mr. Flag just looked confused and reached awkwardly up to touch his nose. Joe ran. He took off to his next class and sat there trembling. He'd called Mr. Flag pig nose and now he had one. What was happening? The whole day had been bad. The rest of the day passed slowly with Joe trying to figure out what happened. The whole school was talking about Mr. Flag. It seemed he'd gone to a doctor at lunch break and returned with a huge bandage on his nose, but everyone claimed his nose still looked the same. When the bell rang for dismissal, Joe was the first one out the door. When he arrived at home, he went straight home and finished his homework. When Mom called him for supper, he ate and then returned directly to his room. He had a lot of thinking to do. He spent maybe five minutes finding out that his Mom had not been yelling at him this morning and then went to bed early.

The next day Joe was determined to fix everything if he could. He was going to wish Mr. Flag's nose back to normal and then he was going to keep the artifact to wish for some good things for his family. Then, he'd replace it before the items were returned to the museum, that is if the thing really was magic. He would soon know.

In the middle of Social Studies class, Joe rubbed the gold pen and wished for Mr. Flag's nose to return to normal. A flash of light lit the room for a moment and then for the first time that morning Mr. Flag spoke.

"Oh, thank God," he said yanking the bandage off his nose. "O.K. class, you can stop reading. We have some real work to do."

Thank God, Joe thought. He hadn't liked Mr. Flag but much rather liked his teasing and yelling rather than the solemn faced character who sat and watched them read all morning.

At lunch a food fight developed without any help from Joe but naturally he was going to have fun too, so he heaved a whole cup of chocolate pudding at his friend Tommy just as the cafeteria monitor walked in. Tommy started crying because he had pudding in his eyes. Miss Cori was furious. She sent someone to take Tommy to the nurse. Then she grabbed Joe's arm.

"You have detention tonight. One hour for throwing food in the cafeteria."

"But I didn't start it, all the other kids were throwing stuff"—

"But I saw you," Miss Cori hissed, "and you're the one to stay tonight."

Old bitch thought Joe as he watched her walk away. I hope she falls and breaks a leg. That familiar flash of light lit the room and Joe watched Miss Cori slip and fall on the piles of pudding still on the floor which had blinded Tommy.

"Oh, Oh," she yelled. "Someone get the nurse. I think I broke my leg." Several teachers rushed in and an ambulance was called. Miss Cori was sent to the hospital—diagnosis broken leg. "Oh no." thought Joe. "I've done it again. I have to get rid of this thing. He ran into the boy's bathroom and stared at it. On the bottom the number had changed. He didn't know what it had said at first but now he had no doubts. The Roman numeral 7 was there. That must mean he had seven wishes left. I have to get rid of this, he thought. He sneaked into the art room and placed the pen back on the display, then ran as fast as he could but when he reached his next class, the golden pen was still in his pocket. Now he understood it would remain there until all the wishes were gone. He felt trapped. Before the last class that day, Joe was called into the office.

"Joe, you will not have detention today. Miss Cori is in the hospital and will remain there at least a week. She'll decide then if you still must make up that decision."

Joe was almost in tears as he walked home that day. Miss Cori was his favorite teacher. She was the art teacher and he loved art. Now she'd be gone a week, maybe longer and that dreaded pen was still in his pocket. He tried to put it back and it was still in his pocket. Would this problem never end?

For several days Joe went to school just getting through the days. He hardly spoke. He didn't want to say the wrong thing with that pen in his pocket so he said nothing. Then the news came out that Miss Cori wasn't getting better. It seemed the break had caused her great emotional distress as well as pain and the doctors were worried if she didn't perk up soon, she might even die. Joe went straight to the boy's bathroom, and took the little pen from his pocket.

"I wish," he said that Miss Cori gets completely well again. Then he returned to class.

When Miss Cori returned to school, she told Joe he could forget about detention. She was so happy to be well again she didn't care about anything.

Joe was getting worried. The artifacts were being returned in two weeks and he couldn't return the one he'd taken and he was afraid to use up the wishes. Wait, he could wish for money. How could that backfire? He needed five dollars for a field trip. He'd wish for money. That evening he wished.

"I wish that I had all the money I need," and then he waited for scads of money to appear. He waited five minutes and nothing happened. I knew it, he thought. It doesn't work anymore. But when he reached into his pocket to return the pen there lay a crisp five dollar bill. Oh, no he wished for the money he needed, not what he wanted and he received it exactly five dollars. Joe went to bed very angry that night.

The next morning in Mr. Flag's class another calamity arose.

"I know you all have the assignment I gave you last week. It was due today. Anyone who doesn't have it will get two zero's in my grade book and that could give some of you F's," he said looking straight at Joe.

"Oh, no" thought Joe, "I forgot to do it." He opened his notebook and there it was. A couple paragraphs he'd written two weeks ago on the American Indian. Mr. Flag was going row by row collecting the reports. In just a few minutes he'd be to Joe's desk. Joe grabbed the magic artifact and wished. "Give me a full report on the American Indians for Mr. Flag, please." A flash of light zipped across the room and there in his notebook was a full report in his own writing and in a folder including illustrations. Mr. Flag stopped when he saw that flash of light. He remembered it from before. But it seemed his nose and everything else was intact, so he continued collecting reports. When he reached Joe's desk, he picked up the neatly bound report.

"This is your work?" he asked Joe. "Well, you certainly are improving. I'm surprised you even remembered to do it. You saved yourself this time."

Joe breathed a sigh of relief as he continued on, but now he'd wasted another wish. He was down to four now Well at least it had saved his butt this time.

The next week Miss Cori initiated something new that really interested Joe. There was going to be an art contest. You could draw anything you wanted and color it with the paint provided. A famous artist was going to come in and judge the pictures. If your picture won, you'd receive a blue ribbon and A's for the rest of the year in art.

Joe knew he could win this. He was terrific in art. He already knew what he was going to draw. A dragon with outspread wings. He talked about it for days until one day Allie his sister said, "we're tired of hearing about that dumb old dragon."

Joe got very angry but he said nothing else.

The next day they started their pictures. By the end of the week everyone had finished. Miss Cori walked through the class and surveyed the pictures.

"Well," she said. "You are all very good but the two best ones in my opinion, are Joe's dragon and Rueben's eagle, but Mr. Arkin will pick the best. He'll be here Monday. Now Joe was worried again. Supposing he wouldn't win. He had to win. He had to. He'd bragged to everyone he knew how he was going to win.

On Monday when Mr. Arkin came in, all the pictures were hung in the school hallway. Mr. Arkin walked down slowly gazing at each picture. When he reached Rueben's picture, he stopped. "This is very good," he told Miss Cori. I like this one very much. Joe bit his lip. "Oh no," he thought. Don't let him pick that one. Then Mr. Arkin moved on to Joe's picture.

"This one is very good, too, he said. "I'll let you know my decision this afternoon."

Joe wanted to win. He reached in his pocket and wished. "Please let Mr. Arkin pick my picture, please."

Joe was also worried about his music class. He'd chosen to play the trumpet, but everyone sounded better than him. He could play the right notes but he couldn't get them to sound like a song. So during today's session he reached into his jacket pocket and wised, "please let me play as well as everyone else."

Then there was that now familiar flash of light and he was actually playing a song.

Mr. Franz looked up in disbelief, "why Joe that's simply wonderful. Keep up the good work."

But the next session he was back to struggling and single notes again and Joe realized this little artifact was not what it seemed to be. He settled down after that and worked hard on his playing which did in time improve on its own. He realized he only had two wishes left. Just two and he really had nothing to show for having had the magic pen. Well, he argued at least I have an A in art.

Going to school the next day, Joe argued all the way with Allie. His nerves were bad since he'd picked up the pen. He just wanted to give it back but he had to make two more wishes. Luckily the museum had extended the time the school could keep the artifacts so there was no worry about that. He'd been going to school two months now and all he could remember was one crisis after another. He was having trouble sleeping and was more irritable every day.

This morning he was angrier than ever because he'd been playing his X-Box just before school. He'd gotten pretty far and Allie had unplugged him before he had a chance to save it.

"Mom says we have to leave," she said and ran when Joe threw a pillow at her.

In the car they bickered all the way, until Joe in a spasm of anger shouted, "I HOPE MOM SMASHES INTO A TRUCK AND KILLS YOU."

Not till he saw the little flash of light did Joe realize what he'd done.

"No," he whispered, "I take it back."

But it was too late. Around the corner a huge truck appeared coming fast straight at them. Joe heard his Mom scream and then a loud crash and then blackness.

Several days later Joe woke up in the hospital. At first, he didn't know where he was. Then he remembered everything. He opened his mouth to yell and suddenly there was his dad looking over him.

"Wondered when you were going to wake up buddy. Good to see those eyes again. How do you feel?"

Joe's lip trembled, "Where's Mom?" He asked.

"Didn't make it," he said. "Allie either. But you got me, Joe. I'll take care of you."

Joe started screaming and then the nurse ran in and gave him a shot. He fell asleep where he dreamed of trucks flying at him over and over him again. When Joe woke up again he said nothing. He laid there and let the nurses take care of him and his Dad talk to him. But he felt dead inside. He stared at dismal white ceiling hour after hour wishing he'd never seen that horrible gold pen. When his father started talking about home, he panicked. He wanted his Mom.

Then one evening when everyone was gone, he thought about the artifact. I had one wish left, he thought. One wish left. I can bring them back. He hobbled to the closet. The pants he'd been wearing in the crash were still there. Blood stained as they were he hated to touch them, but he reached tentatively in the pocket. There it was, the gold Isis pen but now it was in two pieces. It had broken in the crash.

Joe carried it back to his bed. Oh no he thought. Suppose it won't work. Frantically he searched the room for some tape. He found one in an empty drawer and gave a little yelp of glee. His first one in a week. Then he taped then pen together patiently making sure that each end fit together. Then he held it tightly in his hand.

"I wish Allie and Mom alive again, Please," he whispered with tears in his eyes. Nothing happened. Nothing, no flash of light, nothing. Oh Joe thought it must be broken.

Then suddenly it moved in his hand. The little statue reattached itself and began to glow and the tiny Isis spoke:

YOU HAVE EVERYTHING YOU NEED TO WISH ON ME IS JUST FOR GREED

Then a huge flash of light lit up the room. Joe fell into darkness and then he heard Allie calling,

"Joe, get up. You're going to be late for your first day of school. Joe leaped out of bed and ran into the hall. He grabbed Allie and hugged her hard. She hugged him back and then said, "What's with you? You better get dressed. Mom's going to have a fit."

Mom, he thought Mom he ran downstairs and hugged her. "What's with you today?" She said smiling.

"Oh nothing," said Joe, "I just found out I have everything I need."

THE LITTLE PRINCESS

Once upon a time in a land far away there lived a King and a Queen who ruled over a barren, dry village. The people tried valiantly to grow things in the hard dry soil, but nothing grew. Each of the villagers had a few animals but even the animals were thin for there were only a few sprigs of grass for them to nibble on.

The people were starving. They were forced to eat peanut butter and bread every day and the few fish they could catch in the lake, even the heads. They couldn't afford to waste anything.

Then one day great news was heard over the land. Queen Kelley was going to have a baby. Most of the people didn't care. They were sad because life was so hard, that is until the night Princess Rebecca was born. That night it rained and rained, and in the morning, there was green grass everywhere. All the seeds that people had planted over the years grew up in one night. The barren village had grown prosperous, and it was all due to the birth of the Princess Rebecca.

Several years later, little Rebecca was big enough to play in the courtyard which surrounded the castle. She loved to play with the castle cats Sophie, Josie, Lilly, and Rocco. She had a little table with four chairs and she would place a cat in each chair and then serve them tea.

One day Rebecca decided she wanted a human to play with. She could hear the children playing down below in the village. So, one day she simply wished for another little girl to play with. That very day the stable keeper moved his family to one of the cottages near the castle and they had a little girl named Maria.

Maria and Rebecca played together everyday. They had great fun, but Rebeca often wondered what lay beyond the huge gate which surrounded the courtyard. It was always kept locked.

One day, Maria had to go shopping with her mother. Rebecca was playing alone when the stable master brought the horses back from their daily run to their stable at the far end of the courtyard. He was hot and tired and didn't make sure the gate lath was in place.

"Hello, Miss Rebecca," he called as he hurried the horses away.

After he'd disappeared, a strong wind rattled the gate and the latch fell free leaving the gate fall open. Rebecca walked slowly over to the gate. She had never been outside before unless with her parents. Then, she could only peep out the window of the carriage. She wanted to see what lay beyond the big gate even if it was forbidden. She pushed the gate open and ventured out. The pathway was lined with flowers. It was beautiful.

"I'll just pick some flowers for Mommy," she said as she wandered down the path.

The next time she looked up there were enormous trees overhead. Rebecca could no longer see the castle. Oh no, she thought. Now I'm lost. She started crying and so did the sky. The sun disappeared and rain began to fall. Soon she stopped crying. That wouldn't help. She had to go home. Just as suddenly the sun came out again. She began walking again.

Ahead of her a tiny squirrel was struggling valiantly trying to carry three acorns. When she approached, he bowed.

"Princess Rebecca," he said. "What are you doing in The Enchanted Forest?"

Rebecca gasped, "how can you talk? You're a squirrel."

"I can talk because you are in The Enchanted Forest."

"I'm lost," said Rebecca. "I want to go home. I'm very hungry."

"Well," the squirrel said, "there's an apple tree right over there. I'll shake some apples off for you and you'll be all set."

"O.K." said Rebecca, but I still want to go home."

"Little Princess," said the squirrel, "you don't know it yet, but you have the power to do anything you want to do."

"What?" said Rebecca. "What do you mean?"

"Nothing," said the squirrel. "I'll get those apples."

Later when Rebecca had eaten her apples and found a small cave to sleep in, she felt very sad and alone. All the little forest animals came out to keep her company.

"It's the Princess," they whispered among themselves. "We must keep her safe."

They all huddled around the face of her cave. Rabbits, raccoons, squirrels, even the tiny mice and talked to her till she fell asleep. Then they all went home to bed.

The next morning, a hungry fox saw little Rebecca just leaving her cave.

"What a nice morsel the princess would make," he growled.

He started to follow her. When Rebecca reached the clear blue lake and was busy washing her face, the fox leaped at her.

Rebecca looked up and lifted her hand.

"Go away, Mr. Fox," she said "and don't ever come back."

The Fox disappeared. He found himself in another country.

"Oh man," said the Fox.

Rebecca went on washing her hands. Well that was strange, she thought, he just disappeared.

Meanwhile back at the castle, the King and Queen sent all the knights out to look for Rebecca and had the whole country searching. They were very upset. Meanwhile, Rebecca was getting very hungry. She sat down tiredly on a grassy spot.

"I wish I had some spareribs," she said angrily and low and behold a plate of ribs appeared.

Rebecca laughed. This was great.

"I wish I had a glass of milk too," she said.

It appeared right beside her on the ground. Why it was almost as if she had magic. Rebecca thought back. She wished for a friend, and she met Maria. She wished away Mr. Fox and he disappeared. She wished for food and it just appeared. Maybe I do have magic. Then she got a brilliant idea. She stood in the middle of the path.

"I wish," she said that I was home.

And just like that, she was back home in her own bedroom. Her mother had been standing looking out the window and suddenly Rebecca was there.

"Oh, Honey, where've you been?" she said. "We were so worried. Daddy and I."

"I just got locked in the dungeon by mistake," said Rebecca. "I just got out now."

"Well, little princess for coming home safely, as a reward, you can have anything you want."

Little Rebecca smiled a secret smile. "I know, Mommy," she said.

And the little princess and her Mommy and Daddy lived happily ever after.

THE MAGIC PIANO

Becca and Maria were playing in their new pool. It was shy blue with big pictures of SpongeBob on the bottom. Now Maria and Becca were playing submarine as they crawled across the bottom then popping up when they reached the end of the pool. Now they were throwing toys in the pool to see who could retrieve it first.

Suddenly the door opened.

"Becca, Becca, come in. It's time for you to practice your piano lesson," Mommy called.

Oh no, thought Becca. She was having fun. She didn't want to practice that old piano now. Defiantly, she stuck her head under water.

"Becca," her mother called louder. "I know you heard me. Come in and get dried off."

"There's no one to watch Maria," Becca called back.

"I'm here," Daddy said appearing from behind the house. "You go in. I'll watch Maria."

Becca climbed slowly out of the pool. Very slowly she walked into the house and changed out of her swimming suit. She hated that old piano. She'd been practicing three weeks and still couldn't play one song. Just notes.

Soon she was seated at the piano. Her teacher showed her a paper. "Now these are the notes you'll be learning today," she said.

"Notes, can't I play a song?" asked Becca.

"Well, when you learn all the notes, you will play a song," said the teacher with a smile. "Now practice these until you have them perfect."

Becca played the notes until she had them perfect. Then the teacher Miss peach gave her another set of notes to learn. Becca gave her a dirty look, but she practiced the new notes over and over.

Finally the teacher said, "you've done very well today, Becca. In a couple of weeks you'll be playing songs. Well, see you next week, Honey." Then she gave Becca a little pat on the back.

"Stupid old piano," said Becca. "I wish I never started taking piano lessons." Now it was too late to swim any more. It was time to eat dinner.

Daddy and Maria were already seated at the dining table, so Becca climbed in her chair and waited for Mommy to say grace.

After dinner, Becca showed Mommy and Daddy her report card. She had all A's. They were so pleased.

"Becca, you are simply amazing," Daddy said.

Now Becca thought I'll tell them.

"Daddy, I don't want to play the piano anymore," she said.

"Why not?" asked dad.

"Because I practice and practice and can't play a song."

"But you will, you just have to have patience." said Dad but Becca just sighed.

The next day the class was putting on a play and all the parents were invited. School would be over the next day and Becca was sorry about not seeing her friends over the summer. She was happy about the play though. It was about a little boy who had a lot of hats to sell. All the children had fun playing monkeys. Then they sang some songs but there was still time left so the teacher asked, "can anyone play the piano?"

Almost all the hands shot up but then the teacher said, "I mean play a whole song for our audience."

All the hands went down except Becca who'd been watching a squirrel in the tree just outside the window.

"Why Becca, that's right. You take lessons Could you play a song for our parents?" "Come Becca, you'll do great. You can play a song for our audience."

Before she knew it Becca was seated at the piano. What was she going to do? All she could play were chords. Now everything got quiet. They were waiting for her to play.

Becca placed her hands on the keys.

"Please, piano," she whispered. "Play a song please." She placed her hands on the keys and the piano played very clearly and very beautifully Twinkle, Twinkle Little star. It sounded wonderful. Becca couldn't believe it. When she finished everyone clapped.

"Oh, thank you piano," she whispered.

"Soon," whispered the piano back, "if you keep your lessons, you'll be playing like that yourself."

So little Becca kept taking her piano lessons and in a couple of weeks she played the song again, but this time all by herself.

The end

THE MAGIC FISH

Becca was estatic. She was going to visit her grandparent's house who lived on a farm. She couldn't wait. Every night she'd think what she could do there and though she would miss Mommy and Daddy, she couldn't wait to go. Finally, the day came. Daddy and Mommy drove her down to Grandma's house in New Jersey.

Becca loved her grandparents' farm. It was a huge place with green grass and a brook and even a garden her grandmother had planted behind the house. In the garden, she grew tomatoes, and peppers, carrots and even lettuce. Across the way sat an old log cabin where Grandma's mother use to live. Now it was empty, but it looked brand new. There were no animals anymore except a couple of chickens that would follow Becca whenever she went near them.

On the first day, she helped Grandma pick strawberries from the strawberry bushes. Then they went in the house and she and Grandma made two delicious strawberry pies. Becca ate as many strawberries as she washed, and she enjoyed the afternoon of pie making immensely.

The next day, Pop asked Becca if she like to go fishing.

"Of course," yelled Becca. "Can I wear my swimming suit?"

"You bet," said Pop Pop and off they went.

Becca had a little pole with a picture of Ariel on the handle. They sat down at the old brook for a whole hour before they got a nibble. Then Pop Pop landed a small trout. Becca got a bite too but it ate her worm and swam away.

"Looks like a slow day," Pop Pop said rolling up his line.

"Let's stay a little longer, please," said Becca.

Suddenly their was a huge jerk on her line. Becca grabbed the pole hard.

"Pop Pop," she yelled. "I caught a fish."

Now the line was zigzagging across the water as the fish tried to get away. Poor Becca held on tight but her little pole was bending.

"I'll help you," said Pop Pop and between the two of them they pulled an enormous fish up on the bank.

This was no ordinary fish. It stared at them out of big round red eyes and then it said "IF YOU LET ME GO, I WILL GIVE YOU THREE WISHES. I AM AN ENCHANTED FISH AND I CAN GRANT YOU THE WISHES BUT YOU HAVE TO LET ME GO."

Becca just stared. But Pop Pop said, "this must be a magic fish. I think we should do what he says."

So with Becca's help they lifted the huge fish and threw him back in.

He flipped his huge tail and yelled "DO NOT WASTE THOSE WISHES. FISHING IS FUN AND SUCH A TREAT BUT DO NOT CATCH EVERY FISH TO EAT."

Then he swam off. Becca wondered. Could he really give her three wishes. Only one way to find out. She knew Daddy had always wanted a deluxe drum set and though he'd bought many cheap ones, he never got the kind he really wanted.

"I wish," said Becca when they were in the house, "that Daddy could have the best drum set ever. I wish Mommy could have a beautiful diamond ring with the biggest diamond ever and for me, most of all I want a baby sister to play with every day."

Seconds later the phone rang.

"Rebecca, you're never going to guess what's happened here," said Mommy. "I bet I could, Mommy," said Becca. "I had a very successful fishing trip with Pop Pop."

THE CHRISTMAS COAT

ed Johnson counted his little rile of money again. No matter how he counted, it still only added up to $15.00. He needed a new coat. It was only the beginning of November but already one could feel a chill in the air which foretold of future storms. He'd had his eye on a military style jacket for quite a while but now that he'd added up his savings, any jacket seemed out of reach.

Nevertheless, the next day he went hopefully to Sears. He browsed through rack after rack of jacket but found nothing even close to his price range.

A harried salesclerk approached him. Wisps of hair escaped from her topknot and rubbed a weary hand across her forehead.

"Can I help you?" she asked.

"Well," Ted answered. "I'm looking for a military type jacket in green or black if you have it. Not too expensive."

"This is all we have", she said showing him the rack he'd just look at. "These start at $59.99."

"I only have $15.00. Don't you have any _________?"

Ted looked up. She already walked away. Ted felt embarrassed. She didn't even want to waste her time on him. I'll go to a discount store, he thought and headed for the door.

In the discount store, he didn't have much luck either. The prices were lower but nothing within his price range. Disappointed he returned home. Later after talking to one of his friends on the phone, he got a new idea. His friend had suggested a secondhand store. Why not, he thought. It wouldn't be the first time he purchased secondhand clothes and he'd never been disappointed.

The next day, he went to one of his favorite secondhand stores. In a matter of minutes, he found exactly what he wanted. Wonder of wonders it was even the right size. He hurried up to the counter to pay for it, and just as he laid it on the counter a tag fell out. $29.99 it shouted to the world.

Ted slowly approached the counter.

"Well," said the clerk, "you want this coat right here. That will be $29.99, and I'll wrap it up for you."

Ted took the crumpled $10.00 bill and 5 ones from his pocket.

This is all I have," he said. "I didn't see the price tag till I laid it on the counter."

The clerk stared at him and his wrinkled money. He looked at the long row of coats still hanging on hangers. The shop would be close in a half hour.

"I'll tell you what I'm going to do," he said. "Since it's Christmas Eve and I can tell you really want that coat, I'm going to let you have it for $15.00. Merry Christmas."

"Oh my gosh," Ted yelled. "Thank you, thank you, thank you."

He threw the money on the counter, grabbed his package and flew out the door.

"Merry Christmas," he yelled as he ran up the street.

The day after Christmas Ted was very happy. He received everything he wanted for Christmas except a digital camera. But one of his presents was a forty dollar check from his brother so he decided he would get his digital camera with that.

The next day, he went to the Mall wearing his new coat but he was destined for disappointment. All the cameras in his price range had few accessories and were cheaply made. The cameras that Ted liked were in the 100.00 dollar to 200.00 dollar range. Ted continued to look through and he saw one that looked perfect. It wasn't too fancy, and it didn't look cheap.

"Can I wrap that up for you sir?" said a salesman appearing out of nowhere.

"Well I don't know," Ted stammered trying to see the price tag. Finally realizing it had none, he asked how much is this one?"

"Why sir, that little beauty is only $59.99. You'll be very pleased with it."

Ted sighed. He reached in his pocket to recheck his $40.00 but when his hand emerged, he was holding three twenty dollar bills and a five. Ted gasped. He knew he'd only had 2 twenties. What happened?

"That's just enough sir," said the salesclerk and Ted walked out with his camera still amazed. Two weeks later, Ted went to the movies with two of his friends. At Intermission time, John stood up.

"I'm going to buy some goodies," he said. "Anybody else want some?"

"Super big popcorn and soda for me," said Jack.

"How about you, Ted?"

Now Ted knew he didn't have a dime. He scraped together every penny he had just to pay for the movie, but still he reached his hand into his new green jacket anyway. His hand touched something paper and crumpled up and he pulled out a ten dollar bill.

"Pop, popcorn and a soda too," he stuttered handing Josh the bill.

When Josh left, he knew. The coat was giving him money. This was the third time he'd found money when he knew he didn't have any. What a wonderful old coat. It might fit a little tight and there were a couple of rips around the collar but no one in the world had a coat like this.

Ted wore the coat every day after that. Soon every bill he owed was paid and anything he desired was available to him.

One day his mother said, "Ted please leave that jacket home today. I know you love it, but I want to get it dry cleaned. Can't have you walking around looking like slob."

"But Mom, I don't want to. I like my jacket."

"I know, Honey, but it's getting dirty and it's only one day. I'll even have the cleaner sew those tears up for you."

After much deliberation Ted finally agreed. When Ted returned from school that day, the first thing he did was look for his coat. It wasn't hanging in its usual place.

"Mom," he yelled. "Where's my coat?"

"Check your room, Honey," she replied with a huge smile.

When Ted first saw the coat, he couldn't believe his eyes. It looked brand new. Then he looked closer and then closer. It was BRAND NEW. This wasn't his coat. It looked just like his coat, but it wasn't this.

"Mom," he yelled. "Where's my coat? My old coat. What did you do with it?"

"Well after I bought you the new coat and you really deserve it dear, that coat you had was a bit shabby and way too tight."

"MOM?"

"O.K., I passed the railroads tracks. This homeless guy was trying to sneak on the rain. He was freezing. I felt so sorry for him and I gave him the coat. He was so grateful and you and I should both feel happy that we helped somebody less fortunate than us. Now give me a big hug and enjoy that new coat with my blessing."

Ted hugged his Mom extra hard and buried his face in her shoulder so that even she couldn't see the tears in his eyes.

THE END

THE GAME

Jonathan Andrews was very happy. Today his mother had finally bought him that new game, The Mercenary. He couldn't wait to play it. He started up the game and from then on it took control of his life. His mother served his meals in front of the game, he washed in front of the game, and sometimes even fell asleep in front of the game. In his young lifetime he had beat a lot of games, but this one was different. No matter how much he played, there was always some little twist that kept him from winning.

One day he was just playing around, and he killed one of his own men.

"Hey, Buddy," you killed one of us," came a deep guttural voice from the machine.

Jonathan jumped. In all the games he played none had ever talked back to him.

"We're on your side. That's why we have on blue uniforms. So knock it off, dude."

Jonathan got very angry. It's just a stupid game, he thought. It can't tell me what to do. I can kill them all if I want. He aimed his gun and fired again. Another blue coat fell. He fired again and again. He heard an anguished scream when he looked up, three of his men were dead. A deep voice emanated from the game: It said, "you've seen us beheaded, and split apart by bullets, ripped to pieces with knives, and now you will become one of us because you have foolishly killed half of your team."

Jonathan reached nervously to shut the controls off.

"Oh no you don't!"

A flash of light exploded from the TV set and settled directly on Jonathan. Jonathan could feel himself getting smaller and suddenly he was looking at the spot where he had been sitting. Oh my God, he thought, I'm in the TV. I have to get out.

"Too late, Buddy," came an angry voice next to his head. "You thought it was fun to kill us. Now you have to take the place of the men you killed. Look at your clothes."

I've got to get out of here, thought Jonathan. He pounded on the screen. He realized he was wearing a blue uniform too. No one heard him. He frantically called his sister and then his mother, but no one was around. He himself had told everyone to stay out of his way whenever he was playing a game.

"All right men, time to return to the barracks," issued a deep voice. They all started to march away from the screen.

"Andrews get in line," came the voice and Jonathan had no choice but to follow them. He followed them across the ugly desert with tears in his eyes, but he didn't know what else to do.

That evening Jonathan's Mom returned from the store. She was surprised to not see Jonathan in his usual chair in front of the TV. The game was even put away neatly and television was off.

"Alana, Alana, where is Jonathan?" she called.

Alana came down the steps rubbing her eyes sleepily.

"What's wrong, Mom?" she asked.

"Where's Jonathan? He is always here playing the game."

"Gee Mom, I thought he was playing it. I just woke up. Anyway, he's probably just playing outside."

Shirley went outside. She looked up and down the street. No Jonathan in sight. She even asked a few friends who she saw playing if they had seen him. No one had.

While her mother was outside, Alana approached the TV. She turned it on. Then she turned on the game. Some horrible, winged dragons were flying across the screen. They were heading into a desert and a bunch of army people raised their guns to fire. Suddenly, she realized she had to use the controllers to fire the guns. Jonathan would kill her if she messed up his game. Carefully she aimed and took out two of the winged creatures right away. Then one of the soldiers ran right up to the screen.

"Alana! It's me, it's me, GET ME OUT OF HERE!"

Alana gasped. It was Jonathan. He was in the game and one of the dragons was headed towards him. Alana lost her paralysis just in time to shoot the animal before it reached her brother.

A guttural voice rang out. "Andrews back in line. No one can help you until we complete our mission."

"Alana," Jonathan whispered. "You have to finish the game. That's the only way I can get back."

Another attack came from the sky as the three dragons that were left headed for Jonathan. Alana fired frantically and killed all three. Then she heard Morn returning.

"I'll try to help you," she whispered, but I have to tell Mom first. I don't think much can happen when the game is off so I'm going to turn it off. Try to stay out of danger."

The last thing she saw was Jonathan's tear-stained face as she flicked the game off.

When Alana's mother returned, Alana approached her hesitantly.

"Mom, I have something bad to tell you," she said. "You're not going to believe it."

"Alana. I don't have time for this right now, I HAVE TO FIND JONATHAN."

"Mom, that's what I'm trying to tell you. Jonathan is in the game."

"That's impossible, that could not happen," yelled Shirley.

Alana turned the game on.

"Mom, look! Look at that little soldier, the one trying to look out the screen, the one that's crying."

"Shirley looked and then she screamed, "Oh my God, it is Jonathan, it is, how did this happen?"

"I don't know, Mom, when I came downstairs, he called me from the TV and the only way he can get out is if I win the game. And Mom if he dies in there, he dies for real."

"Oh my God," whispered Shirley. "We'll have to call someone."

"Who, Mom, who can you call? There is no one who knows more about these games than Jonathan and he's in the game. I know a little bit and I can keep him from dying and all I can do is try."

At that time Alana noticed their weapons were blinking low ammo. Quickly she grabbed the controls and refilled their weapons at the ammunition crates. Now at least they could continue fighting with her help.

"Mom, I was trying to learn the game, but I can't while it's playing. Someone could die."

"Quickly, turn it off, I have to think what to do," whispered Shirley.

Shirley climbed the steps slowly. She got a wet towel from the bathroom, placed it on her aching head and fell across her bed.

"I have to save Jonathan," she mumbled as her tired body fell asleep.

Alana, meanwhile, had learned a few things about the game. She knew one had to use an adrenaline syringe to restore energy to the soldiers and that there weren't many syringes available. She also knew red kill areas meant instant death if you crossed lines. Other than that, the object of the game seemed to be to kill as many of the enemy as you could and when you reached a certain quota, you won the game.

Alana's mother had fallen asleep. Now was the time to finish the game. Alana cautiously turned on the game. The soldiers were passing a little town. A bunch of soldiers approached dressed in green. They were the enemy. Alana grabbed the controllers and had all her soldiers fire until nothing but bodies littered the ground.

"Good shooting men," called the captain. "Let's roll out."

They encountered two more groups of soldiers on their way, which they disposed of quite nicely. The captain then noticed their ammunition was getting low and there were no ammunition crates to refill. Suddenly up the road ahead of them loomed a huge old house.

"I bet that's where the rest of them are hiding," said the captain. "Let's get em."

"Fire the grenade launcher," he yelled.

A huge explosion exploded leaving a hole big enough for them to walk through.

The soldiers all scrambled through the hole and searched the house for any invaders. Jonathan scraped his leg climbing through the broken window, but no one was about to help him now. They had a mission to finish. They searched the whole house and finally found a bunch of the enemy hiding in the basement.

"Fire to kill, men," yelled the captain.

The men with Alana's help fired vigorously until every one of the enemy soldiers were dead and just in time for now they were out of ammunition.

"Well, men, I think we've finished our mission," said the captain and immediately they were back where they started, but Jonathan started glowing brighter and brighter and suddenly he was standing back in his living room again.

Alana hugged him. "Honey, I'm so glad your back. I have to call Morn. MOM, Mom, Jonathan is back."

Shirley came running down the steps. "Oh Honey, your leg is bleeding. I'll fix it. Don't ever touch that game again."

Jonathan looked at the game. Then very carefully he packed it up and grabbed all the other games off the shelf. He walked slowly out the door and threw everything into the old trashcan by the side of the house. When he returned, his mother had bandages and medicine for his leg which she applied wondering why he hadn't spoken yet.

Now he said in a tired old voice, "Mom, I'm going to clean my room. Never ever buy me a game again."

Alana and Shirley looked at each other. They could hear him moving things around upstairs.

"Do you think he's alright?" whispered Alana. "Mom his eyes were blue."

"I don't know," said Shirley. "All we can do is pray." Their Jonathan had brown eyes.

Upstairs they could hear Jonathan whimpering. He was crying.

Alana stared sadly out the window. Had she really saved her brother? She hoped so.

The End